By the author:

My Life at First Try, novel

An Accidental American Odyssey

immigrant stories

Mark Budman

Livingston Press

The University of West Alabama

Livingston, AL, United States

UWA
the UNIVERSITY of
WEST ALABAMA

Some stories appeared in these magazines under slightly different
versions:

The Selfless Quarantine *The Third Estate Art* (2020)

A Perfect Rhyme Translated from Scratch *American Scholar* (2015) as
A Diptych Translated from Scratch

The Titan. An Office Romance *London Magazine* (2015)

Influenceur, C'est Moi *Pocket Samovar* (2020)

Odnoklassniki *The Literary Review* (2012)

The Land Of Dreams, the Garden Of Insomnia *Virginia Quarterly*
(2002)

Für Elise *Blip Magazine* (1997)

Door *Salt Hill* (2019)

Her Time Pieces *Flash Fiction Magazine* (2018)

Love and Faith in the Shadow of Lenin *Painted Bride Quarterly* (2012)

Super Couple *New World Writing* (2017)

Rezoning Nazis Drink Alphabet Soup *Short Fiction* (UK) (2010)

An
Accidental
American
Odyssey

It takes a very long time to become young.

— **Pablo Picasso**

Table of Contents

A Perfect Rhyme
Translated from Scratch

The waitress, who came from China five years ago, likes her menus to rhyme. The restaurant manager leans against the wall and listens. The waitress is watching the lone customer, who chews his cheeseburger as if it's a dish made with $3,600-a-pound European truffles. The waitress is trying to find rhymes for the daily specials. She says, "lamb chops—shooting cops." Then she whispers something in Chinese, and says aloud, "broiled sole—go on parole."

She does this every day. She has time to spare; no one comes to the restaurant except for a few burly frackers who reek of secret chemical compounds and whose bellies quake like the cracked earth. The manager knows not a word of Chinese except for bu hao, which the waitress told him means "no good," but might as well mean "go, play with yourself, round-eye."

The manager wonders what forces brought her here to the small hamlet in northern Pennsylvania by the New

York State border, a place full of mostly white folks, second or third generation Slavic immigrants, and with Native American names like Susquehanna, Towanda, and Owego. He doesn't ask. He's afraid to embarrass her or unearth something unpleasant.

During her breaks, the waitress sits leaning on a pink pillow she brought from home; she says it was antique, from the Ming Dynasty, and she bought it soooo cheap. She spreads cream cheese, straw-berry jelly, and honey on a piece of toast with a spoon, and then licks the mixture off with her tongue.

The manager knows he's a poet, albeit unpublished. No one else knows that. His poetic soul runs wild, maybe even unhinged. He imagines the waitress wrapped in red raw silk, swishing around her slender arms and lean thighs when she dances for her own pleasure. He imagines her sitting in the lotus position, her navel holding an ounce of frankincense, needles dotting her back, incense burning, though that image could have come from another civilization—1,001 Nights, maybe? He imagines her smelling not of the kitchen but of plum blossoms, camellia, and chrysanthemums. But maybe plum blossoms come from some haiku? He forgot if haiku is Chinese or Vietnamese? He has to look it up.

Sitting in his office, a converted broom closet but with a newish glass door so he can see and be seen, he tries to follow her lead and diligently whispers "cream" and "dream" or "eggs" and "begs." That's as far as he can go.

Mark Budman

He checks the online thesaurus on his office computer—Windows XP, duh!— for a synonym for "porcelain," but he can't find a better word to describe her skin. After all, his degree is in anthropology and women's studies.

At home, in his iron bed, the restaurant manager is covered by a regimental-style woolen blanket, itchy and thin. Ironically, they call this type of bed and blanket twin. His pajamas stick to his skin in sweaty patches. Above him hangs a framed photograph of his wife, who ran away with a corporate auditor.

"I like him because he plays guitar in a restaurant band after work," the manager's wife said be-fore she left. "And he writes comments on Yahoo! His handle is Melody123. That's creative. As for you, you have no imagination and no talents."

The wife's eyes that can come only from a nightmare—overly large irises, misty-gray with iron speckles, and bloodshot whites—drill the sleeping man. Because of that, short-skirted big-bosomed women, armed with steak knives and broken wine bottles, chase him in his dreams, and he wakes up with a headache and red eyes. That's been going on for at least 1,001 nights.

His wife was a smoker. He imagines what it is like to inhale smoke. Won't it burn his lungs? He coughs.

Good thing he cleared their mutual bank account after she made this announcement, while she was packing her suitcases. After all, she made only 81% of what he did.

When the waitress tells the male customers about

the house specials, she leans low. At least it's low for the manager. Her breasts—the little he can see of them—are gold diluted by milk. His ears turn the color of the Chinese flag. When she walks, she sways her hips, causing his head to swim. She is taller than he is, though not by much.

Sometimes, she pours herself a shot of whiskey, and he watches her swallow it, imagining it go down her silky throat. Once, he saw her taking $10 from the register. He put his own money in to replace it.

He's never seen her with either a man or a woman. Is it possible that someone is not interested in sex? He dismisses this possibility. It would ruin his world without an opportunity for fixing it.

He imagines her marrying him and tending to the fire of his heart at his home hearth. He berates himself that his thoughts are too patriarchal, but then retorts that his desire doesn't come from the out-dated male ego, but because it would be so poetic to marry someone who is so deep in poetry. He'll buy a wider bed. Maybe bu hao means "my love?"

Later, she tells him about her boyfriends. She had three so far.

The manager is envious of all three though they are probably worthless dudes. He bets that's what they call themselves. They certainly are not poets.

The manager watches a flash of the waitress's legs and the flaunting curve of her spine, and he's ready to flip. She doesn't see him watching her, he hopes. On

Mark Budman

the other hand, she never sees him. Never! He's Mr. Cellophane from the musical Chicago, but who can't even sing. Maybe he also needs to get her something antique, something with a romantic, poetic story attached.

Like about a loving couple that shared a quilt for forty years, who dreamed under it, made love under it, conceived children under it, warmed their bodies under it during the cold nights, kept a generation of cats on top of it, but a thief stole it while they went on their first vacation in years, and sold on e-Bay for peanuts, and now the couple is searching all over the country for the stolen quilt.

The manager steps away, covers his face with the menu, and tries to find a perfect rhyme for "smitten." "Bitten" smacks of a vampire movie. "Mitten" is totally irrelevant. "Written?" "It has been writ-ten that you and me will be together forever, my sexy kitten." That's just plain stupid. The day he finds the rhyme, he will ask her out. But this is as hard as finding a perfect rhyme for "orange" or "silver," which every student of poetry knows is impossible, but which every student of poetry wants to crack.

The Selfless Quarantine

It's almost like in the old country you abandoned a zillion years ago, but more twenty-first-century-ish. Nothing works. The businesses are closed. Your car won't start. The Internet is down. Your phone shows random clips from YouTube and you can't restart or turn it off. The radio plays nothing but "The Star Spangled Banner" and "Hail to the Chief."

You and your neighbor, who came from a country that used to border your old country, pay through the nose for a working van and a driver.

"Where to?" she asks. She's leathered from top to bottom. Her cap, her jacket, her vest, her pants, her boots. You wonder if she wears a leather thong. Probably not. Only babes from dystopian B-movies wear those. She is not a babe. She's armed to her predatory yellow teeth.

"To the Selfless Quarantine," you say.

She grins. "Of course. You and the zillion others."

She pauses and adds, "The world is brought to its knees."

Her own knees are stained. You hope it's not blood.

She doesn't take cash. Only silver and gold. She bites the coins. You suppose she checks them to see if they are not fake. Silver and gold is supposed to be soft. You wonder if she's soft. You think she'd break your teeth.

You run upstairs to get your wife. The elevator doesn't work. The stairs are littered with discarded books, toys, clothing and bed linen.

You find your wife on the sofa in the living room. She's covered with nothing but a sheet of a bubble wrap. There is an old man lying on the other sofa. He wears a robe and sandals, and he holds a wooden staff. You think it's the same guy both of you saw a week ago in the city square. He wore a sign, "The End is near!!" You wondered why he had only two exclamation points. Maybe he ran out of paint?

"He wears sackcloth," your wife said.

You couldn't show your ignorance to her. You decided to look up the word, but you forgot. You had too many other words on your mind.

Now, the old man tells your wife about his youth in the third firmament of heaven. His voice is quivering. She looks at the ceiling and smiles.

Your wife and you were popping the bubbles the night before.

Now, you take a silk sheet from the closet, wrap your wife and carry her downstairs, leaving the old man bubbling. His last words are "shelter in place," unless it's "shelter in peace."

You step over the dying.

A boy about ten sits leaning against a wall. He covers his face with his hands when he sees you.

"Come with me, boy," you say. "We will save you."

He doesn't get up. Maybe it's your accent. You are relieved.

The van's engine starts effortlessly. Everyone cheers but your wife. Her eyes are open, but she looks up at the van's roof. You take her hand. It's not feverish anymore. She squeezes your hand lightly.

You ride for hours through the darkness.

"Where are you from?" the driver asks.

"Our countries seized to exist," you say.

"All of us will cease to exist soon," she says.

You guess that the condition of being a prophet is contagious.

The neighbor's kids cried at first, but now they are asleep. You see a bright glow on the horizon. It must be the Selfless Quarantine, the last safe place on earth. Unless it's a contaminated village set on fire by the armies of Dr. Alice Shadow, the Tremendously Merciful Physician and the Plague Czarina.

You know it's the former. The world is restarting. The optimist in you is feverishly hopeful. The pessimist in you is already dead but doesn't know it.

You still wonder what sackcloth is. They might have an encyclopedia in The Selfless Quarantine.

Mark Budman

American Zolushka

It was thirty degrees Celsius on an annoyingly brilliant, rotten summer day. Vera had just emerged from the bathtub, like Venus from the foamy sea, but ten times more beautiful, the trail of her wet footprints drying rapidly on the smooth planks of the floor.

A teddy bear on the sofa cast a single, scornful eye over the crumpled magazines, the underwear on the floor, the corner fan that roughed Vera's hair like a drunken lover and the cigarette burns on her tabletop resembling the constellation of Ursa Major. The air smelled of tobacco, overheated body and spilled perfume—jasmine. Vera had just finished typing the following passage in English:

Name:	*Vera Sirotina*
Height:	*5'6" (166cm)*
Weight:	*126# (57 kg)*
Age:	*22*
Languages:	*Somewhat of English (with*

Google Translate)

Education: *Some   university   (Higher Education)*

      Children: *Not existent*

      Marital Status: *Virgin*

      Hair color: *Gold average*

      Eye color: *Sky-blue*

      Smokes: *Only after sex. LOL! That was a joke! I like a Virgin! Another joke!*

      Drinks: *In Company with My Beloved and Socially Interests: Do Dancing, Poetry and Good Life.*

Vera sighed. She had to fill out the application form for *Anastasia and You!* Russian Bride Agency in English, and it was a struggle. English sounded like a dog barking, while Russian sounded like music. The English alphabet made no sense. Just look at these weird W's and Q's. Why couldn't Russian be the international language? Russians had Pushkin and the Americans only his poor imitation—Byron. Unless Byron was British. In this case, the Americans had no one.

The "interests" question on the form was a toughie in any language. Poetry, poetry, what the hell they considered poetry nowadays? But she wrote the truth— she used to know a few of Pushkin's poems back in high school. Even now, she could still recite a few lines if pushed. In the boot camp, How to Get a Western

Husband, they had taught the girls that good English didn't matter. Be cute. Show some skin. Smile. That was the bottom line.

> *Self-Description: Beautiful, Decent, Smart/Clever,*
> *Laughable*
> *Looking for: A White Native North American*
> *Gentleman, Educated, Financially Good,*
> *Age from 25 to 60, with Muscles and*
> *Sexy (but only for me)*

Vera, a fair maiden—scratch that, a gorgeous maiden—was looking for rescue. But the noble prince tarried. Why? She deserved him more than anyone else. She was good. She was beautiful. She was smart.

She had to warn him. She couldn't stay a damsel in distress for long. Any minute now, she could turn into a genie in a bottle. If the prince tarried too long, she might eat him alive. She imagined his feet dangling from her mouth, and she giggled. That's OK. She never giggled in public.

She flipped through several pictures of herself, holding them with her long, pretty fingers like a deck of playing cards. The one in a red dress—too flamboyant. The one in a blue bikini—too suggestive. The one in a long white dress, with daisies in her hair? Naah. Was she Ophelia or something looking for a Eurotrash Hamlet? Naah. She sought out an American prince. There could be an exiled prince living in America, after all.

Life in Tula leaned hard on a penniless girl. Moscow was better, but not much. Moscow, unlike her Tula, had its share of luxury, but moving there was almost as difficult as moving abroad. You needed connections, and rich Muscovite men wanted to marry only other Muscovites. Besides, today he was rich, tomorrow he might go bankrupt; today he was powerful, tomorrow he might be in jail on drummed-up corruption charges; today he was surrounded by bodyguards, tomorrow he might be full of bullet holes.

More importantly, Russia looked gray, smelly, and dirty. Life here was too unreliable and short-lived, like a ring of smoke puffed by a stoned partygoer.

America looked clean and Technicolor, and smelled of Chanel No. 5. Russia was the country of ugly *siloviki,* powerful thugs. American thugs were sophisticated, wore gorgeous clothing, and lived in skyscrapers.

Yes, America has been tarnished somewhat lately. But Russia had sunk as well. If both sank at the same speed, the differences between them were still the same.

If Vera stayed in Tula, the only practical way to ensure the steady flow of dough was to become a whore. She liked men, but not that much or that frequently.

Her stepsister, Marusya, had married an Englishman, and now lived in Birmingham, England, in a five-room flat. England was OK. Not at the top of Vera's list, but OK.

Marusya WhatsApped about her granite counters,

low-flow toilets, one and a half bathrooms, Nissan Leaf electric car, fiber-optic Internet, and movie projector. Vera had to share her bathroom with seven neighbors and their only toilet would often overflow.

Marusya traveled to Portugal and Majorca and shopped at Top Shop (whatever that meant).

She sent pics of herself against knockout gorgeous backgrounds of the Western paradise-like Prada stores, Jaguars, polite cops, and houses with two-car garages. Yes, Moscow had a Prada store, too, but only whores and rich wives shopped there. And rich Muscovites married only other Muscovites. Yes, some people from Tula went to Thailand, but Vera barely had enough money for public transportation. Would Marusya send her any dough? Never! Cheap bitch!

Vera decided on the picture of herself in blue jeans, boots, a cowboy hat, and a checkered shirt that exposed her cute belly button. Her cheeks were rosy, her nose was tiny, and her eyes were blue like a sky in Thailand. Pushkin's statue served as a cultural backdrop. Yes, she found an ace.

"Right, Misha?" she asked her teddy bear. He approved, of course.

She cried a bit. After all, matching was a disgusting way for a girl of her looks, intellect, and cultural refinement to meet a dude. But she had to compete against the whole of Eastern Europe. Even against the Ukrainian and Belorussian girls who spoke Russian and were able to quote Pushkin.

A few weeks later, the Agency called her to meet her prospective grooms.

An hour before the appointment, she applied foundation, blush, mascara, lipstick, lipgloss, and eyeliner to enhance her perfect face—yes, baby, she knew how to enhance even perfection. She left the house, walking with a sexy bounce she'd learned in the ballet school.

She stopped for a smoke. She sat on a park bench, one of her remaining American cigarettes squeezed between her teeth, sending bluish rings to an otherwise cloudless sky. She wore high-heeled pumps, French-made blue jeans, and a tight V-neck sweater the color of lavender that emphasized her breasts.

College kids gathered around her—a prized chocolate, a one-of-a-kind diamond, a treasure beyond belief—and a few boys tried to pick her up. To their lines that lack any sophistication, from "if you were a steak you would be well done" to "pinch me, you're so fine I must be dreaming," she had a single but effective reply, "Пошли на хуй"—"Go fuck yourself." If she were in a good mood, she could've said, "You're wise beyond your ears." She understood that humor was an antidote to sex. It's hard to have an orgasm when you laugh. But she didn't want to waste her time crafting a sophisticated reply.

What could they offer her besides their skinny bodies and screwed up minds? For pushy men with a tough skin, and for dogs too, she kept pepper spray in her purse.

Mark Budman

Actually, some dogs could be trusted, but no men. Take her Godfather Boris, that jerk. He used to be the chief accountant for the District Party committee, and now he did the same for a *siloviki*-run export firm. Business probably wasn't too good because the Godfather looked thinner than her "fuck you" finger. He lost half of his teeth, wore the same drab suit every day, and never gave her a single kopeck, though he somehow afforded to buy himself a walking stick with a concealed stiletto he called "my magic wand." When he came over for a visit, he waved it in the air, and murmured charms to conjure her a car, a foreign husband, and a new iPhone. Nothing had ever happened except that he once broke her vase with the tip of his stick.

However, the next time he was able to conjure her up a pepper spray for good luck as well as protection. He was against the idea of a bridal agency, but she disregarded his advice like always.

When Vera entered the Agency building, they led her into a large, well-lit room. Two dozen young women, most dressed better than her, were lined up against the walls. An agent herded a bunch of foreign dudes. They could've been brothers. Most in their thirties, overweight, balding, short, all in dark gray suits and colorful ties.

But one of them stood out like a gold tooth among its rotting brethren. The dude—no, the man—wore a silk suit rather than wool-and-polyester. His massive watchband looked like real gold. His shoes shone like the black marble of Lenin's Mausoleum. He looked trim, and a head taller than the others.

The dudes and the man gave each woman a hard, appraising look. They'd obviously seen the photographs before, but now they were busy examining the real thing, giving every body equal attention.

Almost immediately, the man in the silk suit crossed the room, pushed aside another one who also tried to head Vera's way, and stopped in front of her.

"*Zdrastvuite*," he said, the accent so terrible that she barely recognized the greeting. "How do you do?"

"I do very good indeed. How do you do, sir?" Vera replied in English and gave him her most flirtatious smile. She had practiced it for months; it had to be good.

"Hi. I'm John Norton III. What's your name, beautiful lady?" He had a nice, gentle voice, so unlike the voices of Vera's former boyfriends.

She knew that only royalty uses the numbers after their names. Like Henry VIII. Steady, Vera, she thought. He should be falling into the trap, not you.

"The third?" she said aloud. "Are you being a Native American prince?"

A bridal agent—he introduced himself as Jack though he was an ethnic Russian—led them into a smaller and cozier room, like the one they had in pet stores for bonding with puppies, and left. On the way, he whispered to Vera: "Very rich. Sells something or buys something."

Then he rolled his eyes, and added, "A multi-millionaire! They almost put him on a cover of a magazine."

A magazine wasn't a big deal, of course. They published more magazines today than the pimples on all Tula's girls combined. But a multi-millionaire, in dollars, was cool.

Vera and John chatted for what seemed to be hours. She recited Pushkin in Russian to him, freely substituting random words for those she forgot. She took care to maintain the rhythm, though. He said that he wasn't into reading, but he admired her knowledge of classics. At least she understood him that way, because that was what she wanted to hear.

"I am poor Zolushka," she said in English, smiling with her best-rehearsed smile. "I am being all alone in the whole tight world. I mean whole wide world."

"Zoh-loosh-ka?"

"What is English word for this? Ashella?"

"Cinderella! Your English is fantastic. What happened to your parents?"

Truth be told, Vera's mother had left her when she turned three, and she had never heard from her. Her father was in jail on corruption charges. But truth was boring.

"The communists killed them," she said. "Because they liked America and wanted to emigrate."

He took her to restaurants, clubs and even to the ballet.

"You don't understand his motives," Godfather

Boris told her upon learning the news. "You're like a troglodyte in the cave trying to judge the world outside by the shadows on the wall."

"Oh, yeah?" Vera said. "A troglodyte, huh? Says who? You're a relic of the past. What do you know about reality?"

She learned the word "relic" the day before and wasn't afraid to use it.

Boris sat quiet for a moment, leaning on his magic wand. "If he really takes you to America, wire me two thousand dollars. My birthday comes in November. You have only one Godfather, Vera, and he loves you very much."

"Sure," she said. "I'll make it three thousand, boy. Just keep your nose out of my life, okay?"

Three nights later, in John's hotel room, Vera lowered her eyes, blushed and said, "I have been swept away from my legs by you, John, darling. It has never happened to me before in my entire honest life of virginal hardship. I feel like I am dreaming while I awaken. I feel like you carrying me through the doors of Paradise using both of your arms and your smile."

They had taught her this phrase in the boot camp, but she made it even better. John and she had just returned from an agency's ball, and she was still dressed in a white gown that John had bought her, and her best slippers, polished to a glassy sheen.

"You're a wonderful girl, Vera," John said, lifting her

chin and wiping away a tear the size of a half-carat cubic zirconium with his handkerchief. "Loyal and intelligent, unlike American women. Like a goddess of the morning. You're my princess. Your hair is like soft gold. Your lips like rose petals. Your eyes like sapphire. Do you know I came all the way to Russia to find you? Will you marry me?"

Right on track, Vera thought. Am I great or what? She firmly believed that in her choice of a mate, a woman walks a fine line between being unattainable and readily available. Men yearn for the unattainable, but if she goes too far, they will grow desperate and leave. The right mixture in the manhunt is to be 80% unattainable and 20% available. Now, it was the time for the 20%.

"Yes," she said, trying to remember what they taught her. "I shall marry you, John, my prince. Forever after. By the powers vested in me. Until death do us two separate but equal parts."

John smiled and went to the bathroom. Prostate, he explained, whatever that meant. Probably an American disease you get from eating hamburgers and french fries and drinking Coke.

Vera came to the mirror, a can of Diet Coke in her hand. Her reflection in the glass was an American Lady of the House, surrounded by butlers in black tuxedos and top hats who kept filling her glass from a huge bottle with golden letters spelling "French Champagne," in English.

She would live in a mansion on the hill and boss the

butlers with a firm hand. She would be especially strict with the maids. She knew what they could do to a man. Like what they did to a French banker in New York a few years before.

She would drive around in Jags and Mercs, and buy her Misha a dozen silk gowns and an iPhone 11 Pro. She would run balls and parties and travel all over the world, except for Russia, of course, and all the women would envy her and all men would want to get into her pants. She would let selected few, naturally. Or maybe not. She would keep them on their toes.

She would have an American baby, a real citizen, eligible to run for the President, and she would spoil her beyond reason, but warn her against the treacherous men.

Vera waved her hand to the Lady in the mirror, but instead of obediently repeating her gesture, the reflection flipped Vera the bird. No, really. She did, duh. Who the hell did she think she was? Just an optical illusion, and a piece of shit at that.

She could hear John talking on the cell and was able to make out a few words through the bathroom door. "Healthy… Young… Beautiful… Loyal… Good breeder…"

She knew what "naïve" was. It sounded almost the same in Russian. Did she miscalculate? Was John really not a princely knight but a sneaking bastard like every other dude? Was she about to sacrifice her youth, beauty, intelligence and virginity for too little?

Maybe not all princes are jerks, but I am yet to see one who isn't. That's what Confucius said. Or was it Kate Middleton? Maybe Byron?

She would show John who was a troglodyte, whatever it meant, in here. She would show them all. She would teach men, both Russians and Americans, a lesson. Something they would remember forever. Or even longer. And she'd start with this one.

Vera took off her slipper and smacked her reflection on the head. What happened next would depend on how hard she would hit it.

If she hit it hard, the mirror would've shattered. Shards would fly. Misha would catch most of them, but one, in the shape of an accusative finger, with a stupendous diamond ring attached, would pierce Vera's beating heart. Had that happened, Vera would've said O in a childish, piping voice, and would have fallen backward, turning into a pile of hot ash before even hitting the ground, and well before the twelfth strike of the clock.

If she hit the mirror softer, the slipper would've shattered instead, as if made from phony crystal, and the shards would fall harmlessly on the floor.

The intact reflection would bend toward Vera and whisper in Russian with a fake American accent: "Someone's missing her slipper. Someone's gonna be kicked out of princesses. And it's not gonna be me. Why don't you take your pathetic teddy bear and run back to your godfather Boris, bitch, before you turn into a heap of ash or a pumpkin?"

She would look more like Marusya than Vera now.

The clock would strike twelve.

"That's baloney," Vera would've said. "I still have another slipper. Enough to prove my identity. And you're not a Lady. You're just my fucking reflection and a troglodyte. And you'll stay here, and reflect all those shitty Russians, and I'm gonna go to your country and rule. Na-na, na-na, boo-boo."

Vera would turn her back to the mirror, take her phone out and send a WhatsApp message to Marusya: "I'm coming to the West, bitch. Be very afraid."

She would kick off her remaining slipper, put Misha on her lap, and make herself comfortable in the chair.

The clock would strike thirteen. Everyone knows how shitty Russian workmanship is, be that slippers or clocks.

Scarabaeus Simplex

As Greg Simpson awoke one morning from uneasy dreams, he found himself transformed into a car. Instead of lying in his bed, he stood outdoors, and cars with price stickers surrounded him from all sides. Though he couldn't pinch himself because he no longer had fingers, he was still reasonably sure that his dreams just had ended. He didn't feel scared, just frustrated and a bit curious. Was he at least a Mercedes or Rolls Royce? Since he had no idea on which side of his body his head lay, he figured out that he had turned into a Volkswagen New Beetle, probably 2010 model, the last of this line's production.

Greg tried to start himself, but failed without a key. He could only flash his headlights and blow his horn, which he did until a guy in a flaming-red tie and a polyester suit, green like the scum of a bog, probably a salesman, disconnected his battery.

The timing of this metamorphosis was bad. Greg had to meet his investment banker that morning. His company, ExectoWidgets.com., was running out of cash. And this afternoon Greg and his wife Linda had an appointment with a marriage counselor, so their planned trip to Russia, Greg's lifetime dream, had to be cancelled.

A couple in silk jogging suits that used to be in fashion a few years before came to stare at Greg. The same salesman approached, extending his hand from a hundred yards away. The pimple on his nose, the size of a very large, very faux pearl, matched the tie.

"We are being interested in this car, silver in its body color," said the silk-suited man. "How much will it be costing us, in American dollars?"

"How long have you been in this country?"

"We have came from Russia eighteen months and one day. We won visa lottery."

"Fantastic! My parents came from Slovakia. *Vodka! Seledka!*"

"Вы говорите по русски, господин хороший?"

"Of course I speak Russain. *Vodka! Seledka! Moskva!*"

"Thank you. How much, please?"

"With 5-speed transmission? $19,999 plus destination fee plus advertisement markup. But... If you pay me cash, I'll sell it to you for $19,899. Since you're recent immigrants."

They climbed inside.

This is what a woman might feel like during unwanted sex, Greg thought, vowing to be gentler with Linda if—no, *when* he became a man again.

He tried to drive to his banker's office, but the customer's heavy hand on the wheel and lead foot on the gas pedal overpowered him.

Good thing I'm a car, Greg thought. I could've been a button in an elevator and suffered from claustrophobia. I could have become a slot machine in Las Vegas and have been jerked all day and night. Or I could have turned into a man's briefs. At the last thought, he felt like puking motor oil.

For the next ten years Greg's new owners, Vasily and Olga, drove Greg around the city.

She would often say to her husband, "*Дурак дураком.*"

That meant he was stupid beyond belief. Twice as stupid, actually.

And he would reply, "*Дура набитая.*"

That meant she was more stupid than an average amoeba by ten IQ points.

They were clearly in love.

At first, Greg dreamed about sex, lunch meetings, and coffee. Then dreams faded from his nights.

He relished the feel of Olga's curvy bottom and long shapely legs against his seat and the musical sounds of her Russian speech. They fed him high-octane gas, changed his oil frequently, and waxed him every fall. They took him to the dealer's lot for checkups. He enjoyed the company of other vehicles and watched new pimples grow on the salesman's nose. Greg would blow his horn at other cars but never ran over squirrels, cats, and raccoons. When he passed by his banker's office or by Linda and her new man, he would blow a cloud of exhaust.

When he started to leak oil and a gasket blew in his motor, the couple sold Greg to a country boy in overalls and a baseball hat, with a beard like a broom's business end. The boy tried to fix him, gave up, and left him to rust with another dozen cars in front of his house.

Greg sat under the gentle spring sun, imagining the stuffy grave he would be in if he still were a man, and he tried to show a left-turn signal, the equivalent of a human smile. But since his battery was dead, he could just savor memories of gasoline, motor oil, and wax while singing birds circled above him, mice made love between his wheels, and a family of dung beetles nested in his glove compartment.

Mark Budman

The Titan. An Office Romance

The Titan, the last of his kind—his current name bears no connection to his past—sits in his cubicle, typing away. They hired him because, as an immigrant to this country, he gets a lower salary. He took this job because he likes math. For 5,645 years, he has been hiding from Olympic gods intent upon killing him. Now that they are gone, he is finally safe.

The Titan's father was the ocean, and his mother was the earth. His parents made love slowly, keeping rhythm with the rising and ebbing of the tides. Over his lifetime, the Titan has made love to 3,230 females. Sometimes it was slow, earthly passion, sometimes fluid and quick watery rapture.

His last conquest happened fifty-six years ago. He just can't get used to modern women anymore. They give disproportionate attention to pleasure over romance.

Now, he pauses and turns his head to the next cubicle where Natalie sits. She's a classical Greek beauty, diluted by crossbreeding somewhat. But he's not picky anymore.

It's her birthday tomorrow. The Titan wants to give her a present, to gain her attention. He used to bestow lavish gifts on his females. Heaps of jewels, mounds of gold, mountains of flowers. But now his riches are gone, and he can't afford much on his meager salary.

"How are you doing, Natalie, sweetie?" This is Michael, the boss, that puny upstart. "I like your blouse."

He's leaning toward her, too close for the Titan's comfort.

The Titan scowls. He's not what he used to be, but he can snap Michael's neck like a twig. He can still snatch Natalie from her cubicle and carry her far away from the city before she would realize what is going on. But he has mellowed over the years. He knows that the cops will follow him, and he doesn't want trouble. There has to be another way.

At night, he doesn't sleep. He never sleeps. He thinks about the gift. Most of the money he makes goes to pay the rent and buy food. He has to eat a lot to support his body.

He gets up and studies his face in the mirror. He doesn't like what he sees.

"It will do," he says aloud.

He knows the secret of eternal youth, but he keeps his pearls of wisdom to himself. After he lost several of them millennia ago, and seven more a few centuries back, he has only a few left.

The next day, he brings Natalie 25 Hershey kisses.

Mark Budman

One for each year of her life. He likes his choice. It rings of a mathematical absolute, and it tastes good. The best of two worlds.

She smiles. "You're so romantic," she says. He sits next to her and grins. Michael comes and snickers.

"You're cheap," Michael says to him. "I bought her a box of truffles. $19.99."

The Titan imagines him on the floor, a broken doll.

"He's romantic," Natalie repeats.

The Titan grabs Michael and lifts him in the air like a doll. Michael boxes the Titan's ears with surprising strength. The Titan drops him, but Michael lands on his feet. The Titan feels blood running down his cheeks.

"I'm a mixed martial arts champ," Michael says. "And I'll report you for assault. You think you're a god. Maybe you were a god in your country, but here you're a nobody."

Natalie laughs. Michael takes her hand, and they turn away from the Titan.

The Titan leaves. He gets into his beaten-up Ford and drives toward the distant mountain, so tall that someone high on chocolate might mistake it for the mount Olympus or the Statue of Liberty.

Influenceur, C'est Moi

When Emperor Napoleon Bonaparte first discovered me behind his ear, he had just finished making love to Josephine. So as not to raise her suspicion—she still couldn't forget his lover, Pauline Fourès—he asked me in Italian, "Who the *inferno* are you and what the *inferno* you are doing here?"

"My name is Ivan Ivanovich Ivanov, your majesty," I answered in French, squirming under the royal fingernails. "I'm a Russian-born, but Western-educated, invisible, almost microscopical, but not inconsequential imp. No one except for you can hear or see me, but everyone can feel my wrath if they spurn my help. I came here to advise you on your future military campaigns."

"Call me your *majesté*," Napoleon said, switching to accented French. "*Majesté*, got it? Anyhow, why the *enfer* do I need your advice?"

"Why are you correcting my pronunciation?" Josephine asked. "Firstly, I didn't say anything. Secondly, I speak better French than you do. Thirdly, you do need

Mark Budman

my advice."

"It's a matter of State, *amore mia,*" Napoleon said. "So shut up and go to sleep now. Or I'll send you back to Martinique, sugar."

"Amore-shmamore," Josephine said but went to sleep. Or pretended to.

"So, why do I need your advice, imp?" Napoleon asked again, when his wife began to snore delicately. Perhaps too delicately. She was Empress Consort of the French, after all.

"Because I've spent the last ten years behind the ear of Alexander I, the Tsar of Russia," I said. "I know all his secrets. And before that, I spent another three years inside the ear of George III. I had their ears, so to speak."

Napoleon made his celebrated hand-in-waistcoat gesture. Except he used his pajama top instead of the waistcoat. "What do you want in return?" he asked.

"Just the French citizenship and the title of Marquis de Lutin. I'm tired of being the subject of the inconsequential rulers. And a promise that you will never scratch behind your ear."

I couldn't tell him that the Russians bathe more often than the French and, as the result, several of my friends and relatives had been already drowned in soapy water of a Russian *banya*. And I hate the smell of a beefsteak.

"Deal," the Emperor said.

"Let me give you my first piece of advice," I said. "Josephine knows about your next lover, Maria

Walewska."

"I wouldn't ever guess," the emperor said. "I thought I covered my tracks well. You are worth your weight in invisible gold, my mostly invisible friend. But tell me, how's Alexander's French?"

"His French is better than yours," Josephine said. She apparently only pretended to sleep. "And he's a real chevalier."

"Who gives a *merde*?" Napoleon said. "I crushed so many chevaliers that it's not even funny."

Josephine raised up in bed. She wore a medallion in the shape of a miniature guillotine between her breasts, the exact replica of the one that killed her first husband. "Parvenu. Soldier boy. Shorty."

"Tell her, 'One more word, and I'll divorce you and marry Marie Louise, the Austrian princess,'" I whispered.

"Now you're talking," the emperor said and scratched me behind the ear. "I'll listen to you from now on."

Yet he never did. I advised him to invade the United States, but he turned east. History proved that the Russian campaign was Napoleon's greatest disaster. No wonder.

The victorious Russians still continue bathing excessively, and the English never gave up their beefsteaks, so I stayed in France and advised King Louis le Désiré, Talleyrand, Louis-Napoléon Bonaparte, and lately Macron on matters of philosophy, love, culture, and war. When they listened, they succeeded, so I could proudly say, "*L'état c'est moi*," or using the words even

Mark Budman

Wellington could understand, "I am the State."

Except that they never listened. I guess it's the French way.

So I moved to the US. Everyone listens to you there, if you belong to the same political party, and if you say that the other party's leader is an asshole. As soon as I figured it out, I quickly became an influencer and was able to say, *"influenceur, c'est moi,"* though everyone thought I was cussing the other leader in my old country's language.

Odnoklassniki

In a black-and-white graduation snapshot, Mark, Sergey, and Lyuba interlocked their hands on each other's shoulders. Years later, holding the leather-bound album in her lap like a baby, Mark's wife said that he looked like a lamb.

"Look at these sad eyes," she said, hitting the fading image with her trimmed and elegant fingernail. "A typical sacrificial lamb. Straight from the Bible."

In time, she scanned the snapshot and uploaded it to Odnoklassniki—the Russian equivalent of Facebook. Lyuba e-mailed that he looked like a young deer. Mark preferred a comparison to an eagle, but he would take even a deer over a lamb any day.

Lyuba and he hadn't seen each other for almost forty years, but exchanged messages on Odnoklassniki. Lyuba had never left their hometown. She ended up in a newly created country anyway, when the Soviet Union fell apart. She was an immigrant now just like Mark. Except that she was poor. She couldn't even afford to buy a microphone so they could talk on Skype. On the other hand, why would he want to see an old woman? It was enough that he saw an old man in the mirror every day.

"Sergey and you drew caricatures of each other," Lyuba wrote. "He drew caricatures of me and called me 'Lube.' He became a cop and now he's retired. His second wife is jealous of me."

Mark was never interested in Lyuba. She was too short and he was the tallest boy in the class. "Uncle Mark, catch us a sparrow," the girls had always laughed.

"Do they wear bras already?" Sergey had asked Mark in the sixth grade. He was a poet and looked like Vladimir Mayakovsky, the famous bard of the early Soviet Union.

"We need X-ray vision," Mark had said. "Not black-and white but color."

They worked on that together for two days. Nothing came out of this except when he dropped a pen under the desk, he saw Lyuba's panties. Since it was winter, the panties were made out of warm flannel and reached her mid-thigh.

When Sergey was a cop, Lyuba reported, he slapped the suspects around in his office. He taught law in teacher's college when he retired. Mark had a hard time imagining Sergey as a tough brute. Torturing a suspect by reading him poetry—yes, but nothing physical.

The day following that report, someone hacked Mark's account on Odnoklassniki and sent a Flomax ad to everyone on his list. They should have sent something like eternal youth potion ad. That could get the female part of the humankind interested as well. Maybe not the young people, but the young ones were not interested in Flomax either. They could piss without any help, and could win a pissing contest with an old guy hands down.

"You're becoming a real American," Lyuba replied. "Wanting to take advantage of your friends."

You don't need X-ray vision to see the truth, Mark thought, while not just unfriending her, but blocking her as well. *Those Russians. Act first and think later. Mean and treacherous like their president.*

That night, Mark dreamed of a lamb and a deer locking the buds of their horns on top of a cliff. Then a bald American eagle and a Russian two-headed eagle came and slapped them both. They kept slapping them, though the lamb and the deer cried out, no, no, no, in the tiny voices of 12-year-olds. The bald eagle had snowy white feathers on his head as if he were an old man, and the Russian eagle was sticking his tongues out, and both extended talons, big and curvy like Turkish scimitars, and those talons kept extending and extending, pushing the lamb and the deer closer and closer to the edge of the cliff.

Multus Anomalis

That year Dushen'ka didn't molt, for the first time in her adult life. When she told her husband, who was sitting on the sofa, his nose in his tablet, he said, "Why don't you go see a doctor, Honey?"

He'd never spoken English to her before or called her Honey. As for his advice, it was too late. She'd been seeing a doctor for months now. Not quite a doctor yet, but a medical student. They met in a motel on the other side of town. He was a cardiologist from Malaysia. Unlike the people of her tribe, he was either an American citizen or a permanent resident.

When they made love, he bit her on the ear, then climaxed once, and she zero times. He was perpetually broke. She paid for the room. At least he didn't call her Honey.

She went to see a different doctor, a dermatologist. In the waiting room, she took a magazine and absentmindedly picked through the ads. Every model had such beautiful white skin.

"The doctor will see you now," the male nurse said. He made her undress and put on a gown. Though he didn't leer, she still felt naked under the thin plastic. She pressed her thighs together with all the force she could muster.

The doctor was old. His formerly white skin had turned yellow like old paper. He smelled of eighty-year-old lavender. It was probably soothing to the patients in his youth. He took his time examining her.

"Are you married?" he asked.

She thought for a moment. Her husband slept on the sofa and didn't talk to her unless she talked first. A good salesman, he sold his molted skin well. They had separate bank accounts and ate at different times of the day. They hadn't had sex for years.

She nodded.

"You have *multus anomalis*," the doctor said. "Fairly typical for your tribe. Don't worry. It has no effect on your health. And it's not contagious. Your husband will molt successfully."

"What will I do? I'll go broke in a year unless I sell my skin."

He cleared his throat. "You're young. You can work."

"I'm too old to model, and have no aptitude for skin exports. There is no other work available for my kind. We have Temporary Guest Status. The new creation of ICE. We have to sell our molted skins to Southeast Asia for a living. They consider it an aphrodisiac. Don't you know this already, Doctor?"

"There is no cure for this disease. What does your husband do?"

"He's neither a model, nor an embroiderer, nor a wholesale exporter. What can he do, besides selling his skin?"

"But he will support you, right?"

She shrugged.

The doctor took off his rubber gloves. He couldn't reach her shoulders even when he stood on his tippy toes. She had such beautiful shoulders, her husband had told her.

"Do you have relatives?"

She shook her head. Her parents had long been ashes in an urn on her mantel. Her brother died in the war with the neighboring tribe in her native land.

"Do you want to talk to a social worker? The city is broke, but maybe she can do something…."

"We are Temporary Guests. We aren't eligible."

Dushen'ka bought a sharp paring knife on the way home, filled the bathtub with hot water, undressed, and lowered herself in the tub. Peeling the first welt of skin from her shoulder was 5 on a scale from 0 to 10. Molting was 3. She would get used to it.

She sold her skin this time, but unlike the molted kind, the cut skin didn't grow back. After that, she was consistently lucky.

First in the shelter for Provisionally Abused Females—she got a bed by the window, and only three women cried on any given night, and only two were murdered during the whole week, and no one said "Hi."

Then at the hospital for the Severely Underprivileged, no one experimented on her, and where she got decent meals twice a day, though she kept vomiting after each, and the nurses eventually stopped bringing her food.

And finally, at the cemetery for Our Temporary Guests—she ended on top in the fashionably deep grave for only four people, which was an anomaly. And in the dead of the night, when no one noticed, she kept pushing aside the earth from her face and watching the silently molting moon, while a multitude of women below her kept crying in vain, "Me too, me too."

The Land Of Dreams, the Garden Of Insomnia

One otherwise unremarkable July day, Nikifor Alexandrovich Rosanov, the highest-ranking janitor of the Russian Republic, quit his job at Lenin's Mausoleum. Though he quit voluntarily, he told everyone he was laid off. In another week, he was to leave for a new life in America as a religious refugee. Actually, only his wife Praskovia was a Niece of the Savior, a member of a persecuted sect, but as her husband, he qualified for an American visa as well.

He wasn't exactly sure why he wanted to emigrate. Doubtless, things were way too sour in today's Russia, but this was his home. He kept telling Praskovia the joke about the intestinal worm and her daughter sticking their heads out of the asshole.

"Mommy, look! Green grass! Sunshine! Fresh air! Can we crawl out and live there?"

"No, dear. Asshole is our motherland."

But everybody else he knew either had already emigrated or tried to emigrate, and was Nikifor worse than the rest? He knew that America's borders were besieged by the tide of prospective immigrants, and he always drew praises from his friends for his ability to push himself through the crowd.

He imagined the immigrants storming in, like a mob of would-be passengers assailing the Moscow city bus at peak hours. Mexicans in giant straw hats with guitars over their backs. Latin Americans in tight suits of Flamenco dancers. Chinese in black and white pajamas. Englishmen in checkered caps, lit pipes in their yellow teeth. Frenchmen in berets, carrying baskets of croissants and live frogs. Albanians with AK-47s. Iranians with bombs and folded carpets. Africans with leopards in tow. Greeks with ancient vases under their arms. And of course Russians with suitcases, icons on their necks, grandparents and crying babies.

The night following his last day on the job, Nikifor dreamed of two Chechens in fur *ushanka* hats and pin-striped pants at the back steps of the Mausoleum. Their unbuttoned shirts displayed jewelry worth enough to feed a whole nursing home in central Russia for a year.

"Come on, sweet soul," the older one said with a throaty accent, touching Nikifor's sleeve with his clawed hand. His eyes were small and round, two worn copper kopecks. "We are leaving home tomorrow. We must see Him. What if they shall bury Him soon?"

"Told you, boys. Too late. The Mausoleum is closed for the day," Nikifor replied firmly.

"Here, dear soul," the younger one said and handed Nikifor a thousand dollar bill. Nikifor had never seen such a bill before, but this one had to be genuine. It carried a clear sign in grammatically correct Russian: "1000 *amerikanskih dolarov*" as well as a portrait of the former president Klinton and his new wife, Monika Levinskaya. It was the right color, gray-green, as Nikifor's own face in the morning following a party the night before. Even the size was right—two thirds of a standard pillow case.

"Do us a favour," the younger Chechen said. His teeth were long canine incisors. "We shall be much obliged. We are just about worshipping Him."

"All right, boys," Nikifor said and led them to the back door. "You're good guys. I'll grant you an exception."

He was afraid that the object of his care taking—the body of Vladimir Ilyich Ulyanov-Lenin—was presently alive to lecture him. Lenin had a habit of doing that in Nikifor's dreams. But fortunately the Leader was dead at this point. While the Chechens were ogling and conversing in their barbaric tongue, Nikifor swept the clean floors again, just in case.

"Don't!" he cried when the younger one attempted to cut off Lenin's medal of the Red Banner with a cutting tool that looked like a cross between a Swiss Army knife and a Caucasian Mountains dagger—*kinjal*. But it was too late. Lenin sat bolt straight, opened his mouth, bigger than

Nikifor's head, and cried out, "Aaaaah!"

Nikifor awoke. His armpits streamed under his imported pajama top and his face was wet. The alarm clock next to his side of the bed kept crying in Lenin's angry voice, "Aaaaah!"

Two hours later, Nikifor and his wife Praskovia sat in the soft chairs facing an American embassy official. He was big, even bigger than Nikifor's two meters and a hundred kilos. His blond mustache was trimmed neater than Nikifor's. His tie was the color of the $1000 bill.

"Why do you claim you were persecuted, Mr. Rosanov?" he asked in fluent Russian.

"I lost my job at the Mausoleum when my wife converted to the Nieces and Nephews of the Savior persecuted church," Nikifor said in a well-rehearsed voice, laying down his ace card. He wore his best wool suit and a somber tie. His twelve-year-old son Petka stood behind him, probably chewing gum in spite of Nikifor and Praskovia's strong warning against it. "I'm currently unemployed and my family suffers great hardship."

"How can you prove that you lost your job because of the religious persecution? Maybe you were laid off as a result of your Government's anti-drinking campaign?"

That question Nikifor had not anticipated. He glanced at Praskovia who was staring at the finger scanning machine with a grimace of naked horror. Some of her parishioners claimed that this machine, which had recently replaced the conventional ink fingerprinting, was

Mark Budman

the spawn of the Devil. They said it inserted a microchip under a person's skin. That microchip supposedly allowed the authorities to trace the subject and therefore to make Satan's control easier in his upcoming kingdom.

"Well?" the official said. "Maybe you can produce a witness?"

"I… I don't know."

"You have to produce a witness in forty-eight hours or your application will be denied."

At home, in his two-room apartment, Nikifor slapped Petka on the face with the back of his hand. A couple of years earlier, he would slap Praskovia too, to calm his nerves and to enjoy her ineffective resistance. But lately she would just stare in his face, like a martyr from a Byzantine icon, making slapping her a dull exercise in brutality. Moreover, he was slightly afraid of her now. What if God really existed and was on her side?

Later that night, Nikifor had a glass of vodka while Praskovia was praying. Then he fell asleep and dreamed again.

In that dream, he mounted the steps of the Mausoleum, carrying his lunch box, as he did every working day before his layoff, and entered the room with walls glowing as if covered by jewels. Once inside, he saw Lenin sitting on his resting place and shaking his finger at Nikifor.

"Didn't I tell you not to bring vodka in here?" Lenin said. Then he jumped off his pedestal, throwing away the blanket that covered the lower parts of his body, grabbed

Nikifor's shoulder with inhuman force, and shouted right in his ear, "Didn't I?"

"Sorry, Vladimir Ilyich. Won't do. Just help me to get the American visa."

"Sweet Savior, no more vodka!"

At this point Nikifor awoke. Instead of Lenin, Praskovia was shaking his shoulder. In her other hand, she held an almost empty half-liter bottle of *Moscovskaya*. Morning sun made her ears red.

"No more vodka, Nikifor," she cried again. "If the Americans smell vodka on your breath, they will never grant us visas. How many times should I tell you this?"

An hour later, Nikifor sat on the bench outside his apartment house, next to his friend the Arbuzman. The friend's real name was Vasiliev, but everybody called him the Arbuzman because, in addition to being a junior Mausoleum janitor, he also sold watermelons, *arbuzes*, and because the English word "man" was in high fashion among some Muscovites. The Arbuzman held an unopened bottle of *Moscovskaya* and Nikifor held three peeled cucumbers wrapped in yesterday's issue of the *Izvestia* newspaper.

"Where the hell is Mitya?" Nikifor said. "I'll wait another five minutes and not a second more."

"But he gave money," the Arbuzman said. He was even bigger than the American official. His bald head shone. "We can't cut him off now."

"I dreamt of Lenin again," Nikifor said. "He was

pissed."

"I would be pissed too, if I were him. I'm pissed even in my present in-carna-tion," the Arbuzman stick out his tongue, struggling with a difficult word. "Everything goes to hell. And we, the Russian intelligentsia, suffer the most."

"We sure do."

"We're not proud anymore," the Arbuzman continued. "Remember what poet Mayakovsky said? 'Look and envy—I'm the citizen of the Soviet Union.'"

"Envy, my ass."

They sat silently for a few minutes, watching their neighbor Ivan Dyatlov, a New Russian, climbing into his Jeep Cherokee Laredo. Ivan was wide in the hips but thin in the shoulders. He wore a knee-length leather jacket, like the Mafia goons. His leather boots shone brighter than the Arbuzman's head.

"The other day the Mafia came to the Grushins," Nikifor said. "Brought their own notary public. Shoved a gun into Nikolai's face. Forced him to sign the bill of sale. Now the Mafia goon owns the apartment and the Grushins are his renters."

"I wish I were in your shoes," the Arbuzman said. "To get the American visas soon. Makes me wanting that my wife would convert to Nieces of the Savior, too. I don't mind to be persecuted for a few months for that. This is not the KGB we are talking about."

"No way, buddy," Nikifor said. "You don't want a

Niece of the Savior wife. Take my word."

"What, praying too much?"

"If only that. She's honest now. And she wants me to be honest, too. Why, the other day Dyatlov's son Boriska forgot his Walkman on the bench. I brought it home. She goes, 'Give it back.' I go, 'No way, Jose.' She goes, 'Give it back. It's not yours. It's a sin to keep it.' I got scared. Is a sin like a curse? You tell me. I gave it back."

"Sounds like trouble."

"Worse yet, what if she continues to be honest in America? That's what hurts me the most."

"Yeah, buddy. I hear you. Everything is balanced."

"You tell me. But mind you, we don't have the visas yet. And I might need your help."

They sat silently for a while, chewing on the cucumbers. Kids ran around, playing Ours and the Germans.

"Mitya's not coming," Nikifor finally said. "Let's kill it."

They killed the bottle.

"Listen, Arbuzman, I need a witness. To prove that I was laid off because of my wife's religion. Will you testify?"

The Arbuzman swallowed the last mouthful of cucumbers. "This apartment building is a lucky one. The Grinbergs immigrated to Israel. The Mullers left for Germany. Professor Koltsov is teaching biology at SUNY

Binghamton and I hear is about to get his Green Card."

"You forgot the orphan Vera, the one who married an American millionaire. Rumor has it she lives like a queen in Las Vegas."

"Oh, yeah. Her Godfather Boris showed me pictures. Her—next to Caesar and her—next to a pyramid."

They paused.

"So, will you help?" Nikifor asked again.

"Sure," the Arbuzman said, "sure, pal. Everything for my buddy." He brought up the bottle to light. It was totally empty. The Arbuzman sighed.

"Sure," he said. "I will testify. Will cost you a thousand dollars."

Nikifor felt blood flowing to his cheeks—a sure sign of an impending fight. Yet he understood that under the circumstances beating the Arbuzman up, even if he could manage it, wouldn't help Nikifor a bit.

"I don't have a thousand dollars," he said evenly. "First, The Second Citizen went belly up. Remember them? Then my layoff. We have nothing left."

The Arbuzman shook the empty bottle over his own eager mouth. Not a single drop came out. "I hear you. I lost my savings too when my bank collapsed. Workers Savings." He placed the bottle in the pocket of his windbreaker. Twenty empty bottles returned—one full bottle gained. That was his motto.

"That's good," he said. "It seems to me, I will have the pleasure of your company for years to come."

Nikifor went home. He tip-toed past praying Praskovia, slid under the blanket and turned away from her side of the bed. A few minutes later, he was snoring louder than the Spassky Tower clock's hour strike.

He entered the Mausoleum. Lenin was walking around the big room, his hands behind his back. Nikifor noticed that while his jacket was clean, his pants needed dusting. Arbuzman, buddy, he thought. Where the hell is your work ethic?

"Vladimir Ilyich, I need your help," he said aloud.

Lenin kept pacing, like a drunk in one of Moscow's many sobering houses.

"Comrade Lenin, please ask the Arbuzman to be my witness."

"Why would I want you to go to America?" Lenin said, looking at Nikifor out of the corner of his yellow eye. "Because your bank collapsed? Because you are afraid of the Mafia? Because you fear for your son's future? Not good enough. Your sufferings are just collateral damage.... How will your immigration serve the Proletarians of the World?"

"Because I will join their Communist party and will bring Your Word to the American working class." He thought for a moment and added the words he remembered from his Young Pioneer's times. "Honest to Lenin."

"I shall see about that," Lenin said and lay down on the pedestal. "Leave me alone now."

Nikifor awoke from his nap and came to the bench

Mark Budman

again. The Arbuzman was either already there or still there. They sat silently for a while.

"So, will you testify?" Nikifor asked.

"Will you pay me a thousand dollars?"

"Listen, we worked together for eleven years. Do me a favor, will you? Please."

The Arbuzman looked Nikifor straight in his sad eyes. A tear went down Nikifor's cheek. The Arbuzman hugged him. "Sure, buddy, I will do it. For a mere five hundred."

A month later, on the plane to New York, Nikifor fell asleep and dreamt.

Lenin stood on the top of the Mausoleum giving a speech, as he used to do back in the twenties. Except he had only three people for the audience—Nikifor, the Arbuzman and Mitya. The rest of Red Square was utterly empty. Lenin talked long and loud, but Nikifor understood not a single word. He woke up. The loudspeaker was blabbering in English. A ray of sunshine hit Nikifor's face. In the next seat, Petka grinned widely over a glossy magazine with a woman in a bathing suit. Praskovia took Nikifor's hand. She looked happy. After her crying on her knees, the Americans had taken her fingerprints the old-fashioned way.

"America," Praskovia said, smiling and pointing to the window that showed nothing but white clouds. "We're coming to the land of freedom. We are coming home, Nikifor."

"Home my ass," Nikifor said through his teeth.

He looked forward to trying some whiskey. Tene-see Sippin' whiskey sounded particularly interesting. Or was it Ken-tuki? He imagined the Arbuzman and Mitya sipping run-of-the-mill vodka and he laughed. He might send them a bottle. Or he might not. The possibilities for him, now a proud American, were endless. Because freedom meant just that. Possibilities and opportunities. Such as possibility of following a promise, or opportunity to disregard it. As poet Mayakovsky said, "Reality's now, and dreams are—behind."

"Home my ass," he repeated and wiped off a tear with a paper tissue.

A year later, Nikifor fought against insomnia every night. He couldn't fall asleep for hours, kept waking up, and even when he slept, his sleep was dreamless. The last time he dreamt, during his first night in America, he'd seen Lenin delivering a speech from the top of his resting place, the Mausoleum.

During that speech, Nikifor and his Moscow drinking buddies, the Arbuzman and Mitya, stood in their terry bath robes at attention while Lenin was speaking in tongues, just like Praskovia did during church services. Red Square was utterly empty save for Lenin and his three listeners.

Nikifor had grown used to Lenin dreams, like a drunkard grows used to headaches and nausea.

Now, the dreams were gone and so was Lenin. Nikifor wanted both back. He felt empty without them, like an eggshell without a yolk. He would give up just about anything for their return, except his green card, refugee assistance benefits, and help from the church.

In the morning after one of those restless, Lenin-less nights, Nikifor came to a bench outside his Binghamton, New York apartment. His new friend, Aron Zlatkin, who had immigrated to the States six months before Nikifor, sat there already, smoking his morning cigarette. On the next bench, Petka chatted with two Nieces of the Savior girls dressed, in spite of the heat, in ankle-length skirts and long-sleeved blouses. The girls shot disapproving glances at Aron's cigarette and his Grateful Dead T-shirt with a skull, but he paid no attention to them.

"How are you, Aron?" Nikifor sat down next to his friend. He was a nonsmoker, but smoke didn't bother him.

"So, did you sleep well?"

"Nope. I slept maybe for four hours, on and off. And no dreams. I bet you it's because I stopped drinking. I used to get a half a glass of vodka before the bed. Slept like a baby. If not for Praskovia…"

"Let me give you aome advice." Aron exhaled a ring of smoke and watched it rising toward the morning skies for a while. His long, curly-blond hair flew around his head, which reminded Nikifor of an ancient prophet from a Hollywood movie. "You need to exercise, my friend."

Back in Moscow, Nikifor had stayed away from

Jews. He had nothing against them personally, but Mitya, his former drinking buddy, had joined Zhirinovski's party and Nikifor stayed away from Jews for Mitya's sake.

"They control everything," Mitya had said shortly after joining. "They rule the world."

"If they do, why don't you convert to Judaism?" Nikifor had said.

"You see! Even you are already under their influence."

Here, in Binghamton's Sanderson Park Apartments, the only Russian speakers were a handful of Jews, several hundred Nieces and Nephews of the Savior and a smattering of various others, all refugees from the former Soviet Union. The Nieces and Nephews were nondrinkers, nonsmokers, and constantly praying people. Worse still, instead of discussing politics, sports and women, they just talked about miracles, and the upcoming battle between the Savior and AntiSavior. Therefore, they couldn't be considered true Russian intelligentsia and belong to the circle of Nikifor's friends.

"You're right, buddy," Nikifor said now. "Exercise is good."

"How about getting exercise and making some money along the way? I know a rich engineer in the area. His name's Arutyan and he speaks Russian. He needs people to mow his lawn and he pays cash, hush-hush. I was considering going by myself, but Luba takes the car to work and a bus ride is too darn long. How about us going together?"

Nikifor had made an extra buck in America only once so far, when he was collecting parking fees at his wife's church parking lot. There was a visiting show *Full Frontal,* which the Nieces assumed was porn, in the theater across the street from the church, and the volunteer parishioners were divided in two groups. A smaller one collected parking fees and the bigger one picketed the show with placards "You will burn in hell" and "Would you watch your Mom dancing naked?"

"Sounds like a deal," Nikifor said presently. "I'll take my Phew-Ick."

"Buick."

"No, Johnny said Phew-Ick."

Aron got up and pointed to the car's grill. "B-u-i-c-k. See? Buick!"

"Look who is talking. Don't you know how complicated the English spelling is?"

"Big deal English. Aren't you guys supposed to be speaking in tongues?"

"Tongues my ass," Nikifor said. "I don't believe in this shit. But without Praskovia, I would still be back in Russia with no money, no future and with the Mafia walking all over me."

Aron sighed. "Do you owe the Mafia?"

"No, but they walk all over everybody."

They sat silently for a while.

"Did you hear what happened in Syria?" Nikifor said. "The Muslims killed a whole bunch of Christians again. But nobody reports it. Everything is hush-hush."

"They are only paid to report the Christians' atrocities," Aron said. "By the way, do you know how much a *Time* journalist gets?"

Nikifor thought about it. Between the SSI and the Nieces and Nephews of the Savior's church assistance he was making $700 a month. Since the journalists probably didn't get Nieces and Nephews assistance...

"$2100 a month?" he ventured.

"Nikifor, Nikifor! $2100 a month? I smell a new arrival again! I know it on a good authority that an experienced *Time* journalist makes $4000 a month."

They paused again, watching two squirrels chasing each other.

"The only squirrels I saw back home were in the hats of the New Russians," Aron said.

"Big deal, squirrels! I watched Discovery Wild the other day," Nikifor said. "I saw a lioness catching a zebra. That was cool."

The next day, they were sweating in Nikifor's Phew-Ick, driving toward the rich engineer's house. The air conditioner whined but produced no cold air. Nikifor had half a glass of whiskey earlier in the morning and now his head hurt. The whiskey turned out to be undiluted shit compared with vodka, and American pickles were too sweet for his taste. Yet he couldn't afford imported vodka and he was suspicious of local brands.

"Purrs like a kitten," Nikifor said in English. A

Vietnamese fellow taught this phrase to him in their English as the Second Language class. Truth was, if the sound the car's engine produced was to be called purring, then it purred louder than a family of tigers with a bad cold. But Nikifor liked the phrase. And he liked the salesman who sold him the car, too.

That was just a week ago. Aron had taken him to the dealership.

"I'm Johnny," the salesman had said, shaking Nikifor's hand vigorously. "Nice to meet you."

He was dressed in a shiny suit, green like the scum on the surface of a bog, and he wore a yellow shirt and a purple tie. His breath smelled of beer and Nikifor liked that.

"This Phew-Ick's asking price is two grand," Johnny said. "But you guys look like decent folks. Besides, it's my company's policy to give discounts to people like you. The other day we gave a big discount to a nun. Since you are Russian immigrants," he paused for effect. "Since you are Russian immigrants, I will sell you this car for nineteen hundred. If you pay right now, cash."

"We shall be offering you a one thousand, eight hundred and fifty dollars," Aron said. "And not a penis more."

Johnny frowned. "I have to check with my manager. Be right back."

"Why did you do that?" Nikifor hissed when Johnny left. "What if the manager says no?"

"Well, if you don't risk, you don't eat sweet pies," Aron said in a voice less steady than usual. Sweat ran down his face like the waters of the Deluge.

Ten minutes later, Johnny came. His grin was wider than the Grand Canyon and his eyes shone like uncirculated silver dollars. "Congratulations, gentlemen. The manager has approved the price!"

Now, a week later, Nikifor pulled his Phew-Ick into the rich engineer's driveway, next to a shiny gray car.

"Ford Taurus," Aron said, his voice full of awe. "He bought it almost brand new."

Arutyan came out of his split-level house, wearing dirty white sneakers and a jogging suit, stained at the armpits. He was considerably shorter than Nikifor's two meters but wider, except for the neck and shoulders.

"Hello," he said in Russian. He had an accent not unlike the Chechens from Nikifor's dreams back home.

The rich engineer led Nikifor and Aron to the back of his house. "Here's my garden," he said, pointing to the overgrown back yard. "I like to sit on the deck watching it. It's very relaxing. Sometimes I even sleep here in that hammock. And here is the lawn mower. You can take turns. I'll pay you a flat rate of $10 each. But please move your car. It's leaking oil all over my driveway."

Nikifor and Aron took turns. It was hot, at least thirty-five degrees Celsius, and humid. Small American insects buzzed around Nikifor's wet face and crawled into his body's orifices. He didn't remember Russian insects being that enterprising. Nikifor hadn't been working this hard for a long time, and his heart was kicking his ribs from the inside, perhaps like a baby inside a womb, and his head was heavy as if he wore a lead helmet.

A full-bodied woman, probably Arutyan's wife, came from the house with two clear plastic cups of water. She was dressed in a flower-patterned sundress, but Nikifor was so uncomfortable that he didn't even think of appraising her generously exposed legs and breasts. His head felt even worse now, as if one of the insects had succeeded in crawling into his brain and was building an apartment house there.

Nikifor drank his water and took the cup back to his Phew-Ick. He still couldn't get used to the American habit of throwing out good things. He unlocked the trunk. My head, he thought. My head. Then he saw exploding stars and then darkness covered all.

He came to in the hospital. Praskovia, Petka and Aron sat next to his bed.

"What happened?" Nikifor croaked.

"You had a sun stroke," Praskovia said, smoothing her long skirt with her arthritic hands. "I will pray for you. Petka and I will pray for you."

Petka sighed. Nikifor closed his eyes. He felt like his brain wanted to jump out of his head and climb into a fridge.

"You'll be fine, buddy," boomed Aron. "The doctor said so. It's a good Jewish doctor."

Later that night, the nurse gave Nikifor a pill. He fell asleep and finally he had a dream. In his dream, he was back in the Mausoleum facing Lenin, who sat on his resting place with his hands crossed on his chest. With sadness of heart, Nikifor noticed that the Leader's suit was in need of cleaning.

"I thought you would join the American Communist party," Lenin said. "I counted on you. Why did you fail me?"

"I'm sorry, Vladimir Ilyich, but there are no Communists in Binghamton. We are four hour drive from New York City. The people here are conservative. They vote Republican."

"No Communists?" Lenin swallowed hard. "You have to move, then. To New York or Chicago."

Then Nikifor had another dream. He drove his Phew-Ick along a wide highway, came to the fork in the road, and stopped.

On the right side there was a house, even bigger than Arutyan's. Two brand-new Tauruses were parked in the driveway. The house was surrounded by a garden on one side and a lawn on the other. Under every tree stood a plastic garbage bag with a stenciled sign, One Million Dollars. Men in pajamas slept in hammocks, smiling in their sleep.

On the left side stood a suited gentleman with a red banner in his hands. The sign on the flag said, "Welfare recipients of the world, unite!" The gentleman looked

Mark Budman

much like Johnny the car salesman, just older. His smile reminded Nikifor of the lioness tearing the balls off the zebra on Discovery channel. On the other hand, the garbage bags looked like the ones he used to store empty vodka bottles back home. Fifty empty bottles bought a full one.

Nikifor got out of the car and walked on foot. He saw a tall ladder, all the way to the skies. A muscled man in a top hat, striped pants, and a goatee was holding it while people elbowed each other to climb up. Nikifor circled the group, then mounted the shoulders of the man in a top hat from behind, stepped from there onto the back side of the ladder, and climbed up ahead of the crowd.

He awoke. It was dark. Somebody snored behind a curtain, nurses were laughing at their station, and the intercom was calling for Dr. Luu-eees or a similar incomprehensible name. Nikifor came to the window overlooking a parking lot. He had never seen so many different cars in one place.

He knew what to do now. He'd move to New York or Chicago after all. Big cities have many ladders to mount, too steep for the natives.

"America," he said, flattening his pudgy nose against the window. "The land of dreams. Dreams my ass."

In a few years, he'd become President, or if the Constitution forbids it for some stupid reason, at least

Vice President.

That's a worthy dream.

Everyone knows that reality is just a poor immigrant next to a dream of a newly minted native.

Mark Budman

Für Elise

The day Boris Zelinsky's wife Tamara called him up in his office and announced that she just hired a live-in housekeeper, and he must pay half of the housekeeper's costs from his own account, he decided to cheat on Tamara for the first time.

Boris, a thirty-nine-year-old immigrant from Ukraine, had a single desire: to be a real American millionaire. Unlike many others with similar inspirations, Boris wanted the freedom the magical seven-digit figure would bring him. One day he would have $999,999 and be a slave. Next day he would have $1,000,000 and be a free man. The money had to be cash and not anything else. He understood the logically shaky base of his almost mystical assumption, but could do nothing about it.

On the morning he turned five in the Ukrainian city of Odessa, he came out of his room, in the long pink pajamas he inherited from his older sister Luyba and said to his father, "I want to be an American millionaire." Back in the nineteen-eighties, in the Soviet Union, that was almost equivalent to a confession of manslaughter.

Luyba was playing Beethoven's Für Elise on the upright piano that used to belong to her grandmother. She stopped, her mouth agape. Boris' mother dropped a plate of piroshki, meat pies. His father spanked him lightly and then whispered, "Excellent, Borya. Just keep shush about it. Especially with people who know us."

Boris was nineteen when his parents and he came to America. In New York City, Boris bought lottery tickets twice a week. He won four times, $5 each, and dutifully reported the wins on his tax returns.

He liked plump women. He was a big man himself, six-foot-two, and weighed two hundred fifty pounds in his silk boxers with bulldog faces on them. He dated a fellow immigrant Tamara, whose parents were real self-made American millionaires. And she played Für Elise.

"The boy's respectful," Tamara's father told his daughter while Boris was sitting next to her in the parent's living room. "That's a rare quality nowadays. Go for it. I'll take him into the business someday."

Tamara moved her solid, pleasantly round body of a Ruben's model away from Boris. She had another date, whom she called Flimsy Victor.

Next day, Flimsy Victor approached Boris at the entrance to Boris' house and said, "Listen here, shmuck!" The top of his head barely reached Boris' nose, but his pocket bulged.

Boris assumed the defense position: opened his

mouth, ready to cry help. He wasn't fast on his feet anymore. He had never been.

"I see you next to Tamara one more time and you're dead. Is this understood?" Flimsy Victor said and patted his pocket.

"Understood."

The same evening, Tamara called Boris.

"Flimsy Victor got into a car accident," she said.

"I'm sorry to hear that," Boris said. He imagined Flimsy Victor's body broken by a truck, and he shuddered.

"I just saw him. He's bad," Tamara said. "He's in coma. I couldn't stand it. I threw up."

"I'm sorry to hear that," Boris said.

"What happened, Borya?" his mother said from across the room. "You're so pale!"

Three months later, Tamara and Boris were married.

In ten years, he was a manager at a big bank and had his own office with a Manhattan skyline view and pictures of American West exploration hanging on the solid-teak walls. Tamara was a successful malpractice attorney.

Despite their six-figure salaries, Tamara and he saved very little, and his dream to become a millionaire was as far away as ever. They had to pay a stupendous size mortgage for their $1,999,000 condo, various loans—for his Mercedes, for her Jaguar, for the Italian furniture, for their daughter's private school. They went on vacations to exotic places like Tahiti and Nepal. They dressed very well, or at least expensively.

They didn't have support from Tamara's parents that Boris had counted on. They made them a grand wedding for five hundred people, and showered them with presents for a few months until Boris refused to invest his savings the way his father-in-law suggested.

He tried other ways as well. He bought an apartment building in the Poconos, but had to sell it at a loss because he was too busy to take care of it. He even tried Atlantic City, but retreated quickly.

Once a week they went to visit Tamara's parents, who taught Boris the hidden laws of life.

"Zhizn' prozhit' ne pole pereyti," his father-in-law would say, and then would repeat the same thing in English. "To live a decent life is not as easy as crossing a field."

His wisdom pearls were abundant, like his wife's zakuski. She always tried to find a soothing word for Boris.

"Don't argue with him," she told Boris in the kitchen. "I tried to argue for the first twenty years and never won. Just let him talk. He's not a bad man really. Just has a long tongue. I wish his penis was as long as his tongue."

Boris swallowed hard when she said that. Tamara had complained about his sexual prowess lately in similar, but even more explicit terms. Actually, he was sure his prowess was there, but Tamara wasn't so sure.

Meanwhile, she spent all her time on social media. Facebook, Twitter, Instagram.

He didn't know and didn't care what she was doing

there. What he worried about that she spent more time with them than with him and their newborn daughter.

He said, "virtual life is good, but real life is better. At least, it's more important."

She said, "what do you know about life?"

He said, "I know that real life wants to eat, be changed and cuddled. And some of us want to have sex sometimes."

She said, "all men want nothing but sex."

He said, "real life is half men and half women, and half babies."

Every next sentence was 10 decibels louder than the one before.

That went on for years. They had their own accounts now, and each paid 50% of the condo expenses.

Meanwhile, their daughter grew up and went to college in L.A. She never wrote a single letter to her parents and called only twice a year.

Tamara stopped talking to him. And then she stopped playing Für Elise.

Boris worked eighty hours a week at his bank. At home, he read books about the American Frontier or watched Westerns on TV, or bison herding and Für Elise playing on YouTube. And   Tamara bought an antique quilt.

"It has bed bugs," Boris said.

"You're a bed bug."

After she called about the housekeeper, Boris understood that he would never become a millionaire. He left work without saying a word to anybody, drove to a bar and got drunk.

That day was full of surprises. Earlier in the morning, his daughter called, something she hadn't done for a while, and announced that she just got married and is moving with her husband to his native South Korea.

"We're leaving tomorrow," she said.

"Can I come to the airport to meet your husband?"

"I don't see any reason for that. I'll text you a pic, if you want me to."

"Why, Tanya, why? We love you--"

"So? I'll be in touch. Say hello to mommy."

And she hung up.

Boris rarely went to a bar, and if he did, he was never alone. This bar was called Post Coitus. He sat there alone, drinking one Black Russian after another and studying a big wall replete with nude pictures of anorexic women.

A woman sat next to him and said, "Hi."

"Hi, yourself," Boris said.

She was slim, and she wore a decently thin layer of makeup. Her teeth were like faux pearls, and he could see the top of her breasts when she bent over to him. Boris hadn't had an affair since he met Tamara.

"What's your name?" the woman said.

"Boris. And yours?"

"Alice."

"Elise?" His eyes sparkled.

"Alice. Where did you come from?"

"I am local," he said, closing his eyes.

"Local? And before that?"

"Ah, come on," he said. "You barely know me and already start picking at my accent."

"Buy me a drink, evil Boris," she said.

Boris ordered her a martini, which she sipped a little. He put his hand on hers. Alice smiled. She had blood-shot blue eyes.

A dancer came on stage. Two tiny gold stars covered her nipples, as if she were an accomplished A-student. Twice accomplished.

"How 'bout a smoke?" Alice said.

"I don't smoke," Boris said. "I don't smoke, I don't drink, and I don't fornicate."

"You must be a fucking angel," she said and pulled a cigarette from her purse. "Have you got a light?"

"I think I'll divorce my wife. Or just leave and never come back. That's it. Simple and to the point!"

"You're cute, you know that?"

"Start everything anew. Fresh start. I will go West, that's it. Let her boss around her housekeeper."

"Especially your eyes. Blue. I just love blue eyes."

"What will she do to me if I just leave? File for divorce? Big deal!"

"And your mouth too. Sensual lips."

"Hell with the condo! Hell with the furniture! Hell with the job! I'll get a new job. A new condo. A ranch! A new wife."

"If you're looking for a new wife..."

"I got to go," Boris said, getting up.

"Wait. I wanted to invite you for coffee. Don't you want some hot, juicy coffee to lick, I mean to drink? I like big men like you."

"Where are you from?"

"North Dakota."

Boris sat back. "Really?"

"Yeah. Would I lie to you, sweetie?"

"Do you have a family there?"

"Sure do. All my folks live there. They still have my upright piano I played on when I was a little girl."

"Do you know how to play Für Elise?"

"You bet."

"Do they have bison where your folks live?"

"Bison to us is like squirrels to you."

Boris inhaled sharply. "When was the last time you've seen your parents?"

She began to cry all of a sudden. Boris handed her his handkerchief.

"Get me another drink," she said. Few minutes later, she was crying on his shoulder. He forgot when the last time a woman did that was.

"I want to see them, Boris! But I'm ashamed! And I don't have money for a plane ticket."

"Come, I'll take you home. To North Dakota," he said. "If they won't like your current profession, tell them that you are a Russian language teacher. I will teach you a few Russian words."

"Really?"

"Really. Я о тебе позабочусь."

"What does it mean?"

"It means you're a lovely girl."

It actually meant "I'll take care of you."

In his car, she quieted down, smiling, holding her hand on his thigh. He felt slightly aroused. Then all of a sudden she turned away and began to whistle Für Elise softly. That was the best vocal performance of this Boris had ever heard. Then she fell asleep, her head on his shoulder.

"I am mad," Boris said aloud. Cars zoomed by him. According to the laws of statistics, some of the people inside were millionaires. The majority were married. Some cheated on their spouses.

A few blocks later, he stopped the car near a curb, keeping the motor running and sat there with his foot on the brake pedal, shifting his big bottom restlessly on the leather seat of his Mercedes. He had a full tank of gas, five credit cards and a wad of cash in his wallet.

"What will she do to me? Sue me for a million dollars?" he said out loud. A homeless man came and stared at him. Boris opened the window, gave the man a fifty-dollar bill, and drove straight for the Washington Bridge.

Love and a Few Other Phobias

The husband and wife died the same day, on the fiftieth anniversary of their first date. At the funeral, a thunderstorm happened that was so severe, it seemed like someone in the sky was crying, but only to the people who didn't check the weather forecast.

All their lives, the husband and wife could be with each other only if one of them had taken a Valium or was physically restrained. The first time they met, they sat in a café by the window, he facing the outside, and she facing the inside, and both had to chain themselves to their respective chairs.

"I love your eyes, the color of ice that reflects the morning sun in its glory," he told her. He was hyperventilating.

"And I love your hair, the color of unspun Linum usitatissimum, also known as common flax. I'm gonna faint now." And she did.

They were not just made for each other; that would be too ordinary. They were the same soul, just separated in two parts, like two pieces of a living 3-D puzzle. They came to America from the same country, and they spoke the same refined version of their native language. That's what the husband said, and his wife agreed.

First time they had sex, in her room, the night they met, he had a silk sleep mask on, and she had to guide him by the hand before he entered the door. The silk felt like something advertised in K-Mart, but everything else was real. The next time, he insisted on outdoor sex, and she had the same mask on.

At the shrink, he tried to make a joke. Does Santa Claus have claus-trophobia?

The shrink smiled politely. The husband wondered if she understood the joke. Perhaps it was his accent. He tried to come up with an agoraphobia joke, but failed.

The husband and wife had three kids.

The oldest daughter had onomatophobia, so they never told her what her name was, and called her Hey instead. The next son had Heliophobia, so he went outside only in the dark. The next son had Selenophobia, so he went outside only during the day.

"If I knew it was genetic," the husband told everyone, "I'd have kept my jeans on during sex."

No one laughed.

"It's because we are immigrants," the wife said. "No one likes immigrants, even Fate." She said that in their native language, and it sounded so beautiful to him.

When the husband and wife died together, perforated

by an alleged active shooter's bullets, their kids buried them next to each other in a cemetery with no name, during the thunderstorm when neither the moon nor the sun could be seen.

The husband was handcuffed and had a Valium pill under his tongue, but his wife's eyes were wide open, and she smiled such a lovely smile that the angels came down to see her, but only the ones who had no phobias were allowed, so, in the end, only a single angel came, and only for a second, lest she also catch a phobia and have a love problem for all eternity.

Mark Budman

Grass Haiku

The essence of haiku is "cutting"
(kiru).
This is often represented by the
juxtaposition of two images or ideas.
—Wikipedia

And it came about in the twenty-fifth year of his life on the western side of the Atlantic that Alex had to terminate his relationship with Fancy Beast. While time was still moving forward for him, he posted a "Free to Good Home" ad on Craigslist. He found this category of ads epically confusing. Did they mean that something was being given away to good people, or to the home that is structurally sound, beautifully furnished and sold for higher than the average price? What was the definition of good people anyway? But Alex had no better choice. Actually, no choice at all.

The PETA woman called immediately. It seemed as if she was ready to dial his number, just waiting for his ad.

"The reason for my call, sir, is that we monitor 'free to good home' ads," she said. "Do you know they can sell your cat to a research lab or use him to train fighter dogs?"

She sounded regal, like a Russian *knyaginya*, a Grand Duchess, in rustling muslin skirts, with a peacock feather in her hair, a fading rose pinned to her blouse, and garnet bracelets a la Alexandr Kuprin on her slim wrists.

Alex wanted to explain that this wasn't just a cat, but his closest friend and confidant. He wanted to explain that as a retired engineer and inventor, and therefore a man of logic and experience, he knew the scary truth about the research labs and fighter dogs and blood-thirsty sadists. He wanted to explain that though he used to be an alien, he was now a citizen.

Weren't his English skills good? He could Google, write poetry, and even add an extra "the" that so many Russians drop.

Moreover, he once published in *Mashed Potatoes and Organic Butter Review,* a magazine that didn't charge writers' fees. And everyone knew that any magazine with the 'review' in its name was respectable and hard to get.

He would add that he'd been a small part of the literary scene long enough. Mostly as a fire hydrant, but still…

Instead of telling her this, Alex listened politely, thanked the lady, hung up, and buried his face in his hands. He called the cat in question Fancy Beast. That was a private joke between the two of them, he and the cat, a play on the words on the label of the cat's favorite food. The cat ate too much of it and spent too much time purring on Alex's lap instead of chasing squirrels in the back yard, so his belly hung to the floor and his neck had become as wide as his head. His every step was against the laws of nature, a moving violation.

Alex was proud of the name. A word pun in English, a great accomplishment for an immigrant who had learned the new language as an adult.

He wondered why the PETA woman called. He deliberately didn't use the words "free to good home" in his ad. On the contrary, he asked for a $25 're-homing fee,' though he considered the term exceedingly ugly and didn't need the money that much. The experts said that if people paid something, they would value the pet more, at least initially. Then the cat's natural charm would kick in and they wouldn't abuse him.

After all, his fur was tri-color, a rare male calico. This color brings good luck and happiness.

A woman answered the ad twenty hours before the event. She'd been searching for a kitty for a while, she said, but was always late. Someone else always took the kitty before her. She'd felt lonely ever since her hubby, that son of a bitch, left her, she said.

The woman came to Alex's house with her young daughter the following day, two hours before the biggest change in Alex's life. She carried a large Walmart shopping bag with something inside.

"I'm Alice," she said. "A nice house. I live in a trailer."

Piggy-pink polyester shorts hugged her bottom, and a toad-green tank top of the same material enveloped her breasts.

"You live in a trailer park?" Alex asked, attempting to keep the friendly conversation flowing, as he'd been instructed by his friend Igor, a former therapist back in Russia, and now a stock room boy at JC Penney during the day, and co-duke of the pretend micronation Shvambrania after hours. "Or a stand-alone trailer?"

Whenever Alex's neighbors and former colleagues mentioned trailers, they followed with the word 'trash.' Trailers and trash always came together in American English.

Alex imagined Alice mud-wrestling with the PETA woman, puffing and huffing and clawing her, though the PETA woman still looked regal despite the mud and the awkward pose.

Alice eyed Alex suspiciously. "Where are you from?" she asked. Her mismatched eyes clashed together like two angry lizards.

Ah, his foreign accent! It had bothered his former bosses, but he had overcompensated with the number of patents he brought for the company. It never bothered the cat. No cat had ever been, and Alex talked to many. They loved him and approached freely when he walked in the neighborhood. They rubbed their heads against his shin, then dropped to the ground to show their bellies.

"Russia," he said timidly. He didn't say "the Soviet Union" because he believed it would confuse her. Most Americans he knew wore their geographical illiteracy like a badge of honor.

"I've never been to Russia," Alice said. "I went to St. Petersburg, Florida once. I won fifty bucks in bingo."

"Do you know that when they want to call a cat in Russian," Alex announced, "they say kiss-kiss-kiss?"

"I like the kitty," the girl said. "He's cute. Mommy, let's get him. Pretty please."

"Do you know that cats have nine lives in this country, but in Italy and Germany it's seven, and in Turkey and Arab countries, the number of lives is six?" Alex asked Alice and her girl now because Igor had told him that you must be friendly with customers, and because it was his cat's life, after all.

The mother and daughter just stared at him.

So he decided not to tell them about Igor's and his pretend micronation of Shvambrania, which had no physical manifestation in the corporeal world, but was listed at the *Micronation Central*'s website between the imaginary Republic of Shireroth and made-up Underduchy of Silesiana. And he wouldn't tell about the visit to the MicroCon convention at the public library in Syracuse, New York, where Igor and he, the two co-dukes, wore red, white and green sashes: red for the blood not spilled, white for purity and green for hope. He wouldn't tell about the medals they wore, that were inherited from their World War II veteran parents, and how Igor and he ogled other heads of micronations, but didn't mingle because everyone else spoke with proper American accents.

He also decided not to tell them about his inventions, though that was his third most favorite subject for discussions, after the cat and Shvambrania. So he told neither about microelectronics—the art and science of building miniature circuits and systems— nor about aroma stimulation in digital media.

Alex brought out Fancy Beast's entire paraphernalia: the carrier, the food, the litter box, the nail clipper, eleven furry toys, the sleeping rug, the scratching post, and Drinkwell® Pet Fountain for Cats, and piled it all up on the scratched-up carpet.

"May I take your picture with the cat?" he asked the girl.

"What would you do with the picture?" Alice asked. "Post it on some kinky online forum?" One of her front teeth was missing.

"No, I will just show it to my wife," Alex said. "And what is your name, ma'am? For the record."

"And where is she?" Alice demanded.

"She's working. I'm retired, you know. The empty nest. The cat and me. But she brings home the bacon, so to speak."

"Why are you getting rid of him?"

"We are moving to Boston to be with my kids. They

are allergic to cats."

He wanted to add that the kids were grown up, married to real Americans, and had no time for Alex and his wife, especially not for Alex's life stories, which they called "daddy jokes," and that Alex's wife urged the cat's departure, because she sacrificed everything for the kids, and would sacrifice until her last day and beyond, and that he loved the cat like some other older men love fast cars and flashy girls, but if he really said that, the visitor would think that he were an idiot, wouldn't she? So he just showed her his teeth in a polite American style he had recently mastered to the point of polished perfection.

"Listen," Alice said. "We love your cat, but I don't have twenty-five bucks. What I can give you instead is this antique picture."

Out of her bag, she took a Ramada Inn quality lithograph of a palm tree.

"It costs more than twenty bucks, but I'm out of cash."

When they left, an hour before the event, taking his best friend with them, Alex put the lithograph aside for later examination, and transferred the picture to his computer. The girl wasn't as heavy as he thought at first. Just overweight, like her mother. They would make a good family: the mother, the girl and Fancy Beast, he told himself. The cat was practically purring in the picture. Just look at his half-closed eyes. That meant he was happy.

Staring at the picture, Alex truly, genuinely believed

Grass Haiku

that. Then the screen saver kicked in, covering the picture, exactly half an hour before the event. Alex shut down the computer and went for a walk.

The sun shined, the gentle breeze blew, bringing the aromas of flowers, human sweat, and burned gasoline. The birds sang, made consensual love, and pooped.

In the space of ten minutes, Alex composed a cat haiku in his mind. It wasn't exactly about Fancy Beast, but Alex was sure he'd enjoy it.

> *Your paws weave time,*
> *Oh, awaiting Penelope!*
> *Your Tom will return.*

It was important not to forget it before he had a chance to write it down, so he rushed home.

Then the event happened. On time.

A high-definition camera-equipped aerial drone Phantom A-number-1 that hovered above for the reason only its operator knew, lost its marbles and fell on Alex's head.

The last thing that the camera recorded was his wide-open eyes in high definition.

He died before the ambulance arrived. His Android phone and his digital wristwatch got smashed as well. The drone showed no solidarity either to the engineer or to his technology. But the birds that flew overhead left off their singing out of respect until the ambulance took off with Alex's corpse inside.

They buried Alex on a hill overlooking a mildly polluted river, a trailer park, and a meadow where catnip, an alien plant naturalized in America, grew peacefully next to the native plants like the Black Eyed Susan and Butterfly Weed.

His former co-workers—engineers, technicians, an unsuccessful trade union organizer, and even an accountant—brought him a bouquet of twenty red roses called "Freedom" that they had bought on sale from YourFunerals.com.

His friend Igor, wearing the best discounted suit JC Penney could offer and a $10 tie with the stop sign superimposed over Putin's face, eulogized Alex in heavily accented English.

"That was a bad way to die," he said, "and too early, but at least it was a drone, a marvel of the modern technology, appropriate for an engineer, and not some dumb flower box or a badly installed AC window unit.

"Alex and I came to this country from Russia among your tired, your poor, your huddled masses. Why did we come here, you ask?"

Nobody asked, but that didn't deter Igor.

"Because this country was great. Why this country was great? Because of the Industrial Revolution. The Industrial Revolution made the engineering glamorous for Edison, who was Alex's inspiration. Nabokov, the Russian writer who mastered English, was his second inspiration. And his cat was his third inspiration. How many inspirations a man need? As many as it takes."

At this point, Alex's kids stopped interpreting Igor's words to their husbands. They looked bewildered as if the funeral was one of the daddy jokes, but even weirder than usual. Alex's wife kept checking her phone as if expecting an instant message from her late husband announcing his re-incarnation plans.

But Igor went on. "We both spent a lot of time bringing to the world the pretend micronation of Shvambrania. The country this nation calls home is not recognized by the UN or any governments. You can call it imaginary, but the conceptual concept is a noble one. The country exists only in the cyberspace, but it gives a place of refuge to every needy person in the world."

At this point, everyone present was either coughing or conversing loudly, but that didn't stop Igor.

"I accept, with a heavy heart, that I would be the only remaining duke of this micronation now, and that is a grave responsibility, but a great honor as well. I promise to stand up to it, Alex, my dearly and nearly departed friend. Now, let me read you his poem:

Your name means "daddy" in old Germanic.

You talk to me from horseback,

as if I'm a pope who is defending Rome from you.

A slab of meat is warming between your thigh and the side of the horse.

Your wispy beard

Mark Budman

is singed by the camera lights.
Daddy,
though I left your country
half a life time ago,
I can never escape your reach.
Your arrows
cover the sun and the moon
in my dreams.
All roads lead to Rome, Daddy.
You are coming for me."

A few weeks later, when time was no longer of the essence, the cemetery caretaker, a ruler-thin man with an earth-colored face, noticed a tomcat with a head as wide as its neck sleeping on Alex's grave, under the newly installed tombstone (Laser Modern design) that said: "Inventor, father, husband. In that order." The cat wore a blue polyester bow studded with faux rhinestones.

The caretaker, afraid that the cat would use the graves as urinals or worse, shooed it away, but the cat kept returning, so he gave up and even fed the beast. Nothing fancy, because he was paid only the state-mandated minimum wage and spent a quarter of his pay on cigarettes and Keystone Light. In return, the cat purred for him and once even brought him a dead field mouse.

They developed a ritual. The caretaker called 'sk-sk-sk,' and the cat came and feasted from a plastic bowl bought from a Dollar Store. The caretaker watched and sang the Star Spangled Banner in countertenor, which, as the cat knew, was often broken down into three subcategories: sopranist or "male soprano," the haute-contre, and the castrato.

After the feast, the cat purred for a minute and half while the caretaker smoked, killed a can of Keystone Light, and dreamed of a $15 an hour minimum wage, which had been recently implemented in two states, but not in his, let alone on the federal level. Then the caretaker departed to take care of his apartment, but the cat remained.

The cat actually didn't like to be called by any name but one. Let other cats, hoi poloi, beastly, fanciful, reply to *de-felineizing*, to coin a word, names. But sk-sk-sk wasn't really a name, and he couldn't refuse food. Practical considerations trumped aesthetics and policy.

No, the cat had higher aspirations. He imagined himself The Booted Cat in deference to non-Americans, but to English speakers he agreed to be called Puss in Boots, though he hated anything that stood between his paws and the ground. He knew he was more handsome than Shrek's friend in the movies. Exactly how more handsome he didn't know; "by far" was a good estimate.

As an amateur linguist, Puss in Boots tolerated or sometimes even enjoyed the company of foreign-born humans. They generally had quicker wits than the native-born and were not afraid to use them. As for the cemetery caretaker, his wit didn't matter because he provided sustenance.

Mark Budman

After dinners, when the caretaker had departed, Puss in Boots spent the rest of the evenings philosophizing and cleaning his fur, a time-honored tradition. He'd seen cruelty at the hands of the children and the gentle stroking of his so-called owner, that little failure. But as a true philosopher, Puss didn't dwell on the past, either painful or pleasurable. As a true cat, he refused to dwell on the future. That left only present, and he was content with that.

He considered himself Epicurean, and if he ever had a tombstone of his own, he would have it inscribed NFFNSNC, which, as everyone but the caretaker knew, stand for *non fui, fui, non sum, non curo* ("I was not, I was, I am not, I don't care.")

Under normal circumstances, Alex would have enjoyed watching the cat's adventures, but now he slept through all of this, going native at last, content and oblivious, like a stopped clock or a recently petted feline with a full stomach and a guaranteed life in a loved home.

Puss in Boots loitered around the cemetery, admired by grieving relatives and grave diggers, and even made half-friends with a family of resident foxes, until the first snowflakes landed on the tombstones. And then he was gone, perhaps entering his next life. If he really had six to nine times more of those than humans, perhaps he planned to use them more wisely than they. Maybe he retired to the micronation of Shvambrania, perhaps extending its definition of refuge to everyone in the world, not just humans. Or maybe he built a faster than light spaceship, full of good-smelling mice for the crew, with quite a few warm and cozy places to snooze, and immigrated to Proxima Centauri. He had never seen a Goldilocks planet orbiting around a red dwarf up close before. Or maybe he decided to travel around the Galaxy as an intrepid pioneer and a good-will ambassador, introducing himself as the sexiest cat alive.

Back at the cemetery, unruly grass grew the next spring, so extraordinary tall as if it were trying to touch the stars. And it sang something in the wind. You had to bend very low to hear it, but if you did, it wasn't some gossip about king Midas' donkey ears, or politics, or class, but something that sounded like a haiku, simultaneously in Russian and English:

> *Your paws weave time,*
> *Oh, awaiting Penelope!*
> *Your Tom will return.*

No one bent that low to listen, except the foxes. Even if they understood the message, they didn't share it, though they probably knew that a message not shared was in vain.

The caretaker mowed the tall grass down quickly to the regulation length, and it stopped singing. The rest of the season was uneventful, and it showed all the signs of staying that way. That is to say, until Puss in Boots ran out of his lives and returned for some rest. But maybe, just maybe, a woman would start visiting in his place. She would look regal, like a Russian *knyaginya*, a Grand Duchess, in rustling muslin skirts, with a peacock feather in her hair, a fresh rose pinned to her blouse, and garnet bracelets a la Alexandr Kuprin on her slim wrists. She would carry sacred texts disguised as PETA brochures in her bag, and a magic wand disguised as an iPhone in her other hand. And then the grass would start growing and singing its haikus again, louder than ever. And everyone would hear and understand it without having to bend down or otherwise inconvenience their bodies.

Luceafârul

In a gesture that had become annoying even to him in the last few months, Ion Savulescu extended to every passerby a card that read, "I am a Romanian Immigrant with a big Family. I don't have a Job yet. Please Help!!" The card used to be white; the last exclamation point had long disappeared. One was the right number, of course. Three were melodramatic, but would suffice. Two were a source of a great embarrassment for Ion, a proud grammarian. He could have drawn another exclamation point, but the card was laminated and the ink didn't stick well. On the other hand, erasing one would make a big mess.

This card was the only benefit of the American-Romanian Benevolent Society that Ion paid $10 to join. For that money, they could have used a bigger font. Or write something that rhymes. People respond to poetry better than to prose.

Ion was obliged by the forces of fate to slither in the jungle, rarely seeing a sun obscured by Manhattan's skyscrapers, double-decker buses, cops on horseback, and an unfriendly, overly tall crowd. Even when he glimpsed it, the sun was a source of scorching heat and UV radiation, not the gentle caress he was accustomed to in Constanta, his home on the Black Sea.

Though he wore his bow tie, his crisp white shirt of Egyptian cotton, and his best Sunday suit—the one-hundred percent Romanian wool he had bought on his last trip to Bucharest right before coming to America—and though his shoes were polished to a mirror shine, Americans were apparently not impressed. Ion had done some research; in one study, they gave generously to a man in suit and tie here in New York. That man had forgotten his wallet at home and needed money for a train. Somebody even gave him a dollar for a newspaper.

Contrary to the study, they gave very little to Ion. A dollar here or a dollar there.

Definitely not enough to support his wife Florica—a former secretary—and his sixteen-year old daughter Aurelia, even on the modest level they were accustomed to at home. So they had to move from one friend or relative to another and sleep on the floor. Florica cleaned laundromats for less than minimum wage, in cash, and now was hugely pregnant. Aurelia worked at a Romanian restaurant as a short order cook. Ion couldn't figure out why he failed to collect alms. Was it the missing exclamation point on his card? Was it his hair, still parted in the middle, still heavily greased, and still in the same neat order it had been back in his time as the language teacher back home? Was it his reluctance to thrust the card at each stranger as some other immigrants did? Whatever the case was, he had no other choice. His knowledge of English was too meager for a job in education, no one needed a Romanian teacher in America, he had no teaching certificate anyway, and he possessed no other useful skills.

Yes, he had landed a few interpreter and translator jobs. They paid pennies. When he had interpreted for the International Bipolar Development Forum, they paid him $50, but the check bounced. Then Ion had translated two twenty-page articles from English into Romanian for an e-zine *Fundul de Grăsime*. It took him three days of solid work. They had promised real money, but gave him a lifetime subscription instead. At this rate, his lifetime wouldn't last long, anyway. He even contemplated going back to Romania. That would mean facing the reason he had fled on a tourist visa in the first place: he owed the Constanta Mafia $15,000.

Had it happened to someone else, it would have been a sad story, but since it happened to Ion, it was tragic. Normally, a path of an English teacher runs parallel to that of the Mafia, and the parallel lines never intersect, according to the rules of geometry. Yet the Mafia men had probably never studied geometry, though they certainly understood the concept of a straight line since they were good shots.

One sunny day, too sunny as it turned out, Ion had

been blinded by a reflection in a store window and had rear-ended a Mercedes 500 with his half-dead Dacia 1100. Two men, so stocky that they seemed to have muscles grafted onto their bodies, had come out from the damaged car, and Ion's knees had buckled. He had no insurance, and he was lucky that the beef-men only hit him once. They gave him a week to repay the damage. A week was enough to flee.

The family visas had expired, of course, but the long hands of the Immigration and Naturalization Service were tied. They were busy going after fish bigger and juicier than Ion.

Now, a well-dressed man stopped to read Ion's card. His blue Oxford shirt and dark woolen pants, of course, were no match for Ion's chic outfit. The man trained his green, penetrating eyes at Ion and said in broken Romanian, "*Romania Mare—nare ce mâncare.*"

Ion stepped back, tripped over his own foot and would have fallen, but the man steadied him. How could a human being mangle the language of Eminescu that badly, Ion thought, jerking his hand back.

"Right," Ion said in English. "The great Romania has nothing to eat."

He mentally christened the man "Georgiou," though he obviously wasn't a Romanian, but a barbarian. However, he was dressed better than most passersby were in these latitudes—a blue shirt and dark cotton pants.

Where did he pick up even this pathetic approximation of the language of the true intellectuals, the most refined people in the world?

Two days prior to meeting Ion's meeting with "Georgiou," Florica had spewed blood out of her body, and Ion had called the ambulance. An hour later, he had sat in a plastic chair in an emergency department waiting room, clutching a paperback copy of Eminescu's *Luceafârul.*

A few days before the hospital visit, his friend Kostica Garbaleu had told him that a health insurance policy from a good provider such as Red-White-and-Blue Shield cost $1100 a month for a family through Obamacare. Ion didn't believe the astronomical sum, but he still knew that the cost of insurance was beyond his reach. Yet at the same time Kostica had told him a way around the problem—the hospital emergency department.

"They can't turn anybody down by law," he had said. "If they do, you can sue them."

"Sue them?" Ion had said. "How can I afford a lawyer?"

Kostica laughed. "A lawyer will let you know how to afford him."

So while Florica was being examined—the baby clearly didn't agree with her body this time—Ion tried to entertain himself by reading, but the magic of poetry failed to calm his nerves. What if Kostica had told him wrong? What if the doctors would bill him for $500? Even a $50 bill would decimate his savings.

A brown-skinned man in a white gown came out. Ion's eyes latched onto a red spot on his gown.

"Mr. Savulescu? I'm Doctor Virumi. I'm sorry, but your baby did not make it."

The man to whom Ion thrust the card—"Georgiou"— stopped to read it, unlike the vast majority of the locals.

"*Romania Mare—nare ce mâncare,*" he said and then recited a children's verse in the same broken Romanian. "*Vuesk tractoarele in câmp.*"

How come he spoke *the* language? Ion nearly lost his balance but recovered quickly. He peered into his green eyes. Nothing beyond the ordinary.

Ion straightened up. The guy wanted poetry? He'd give him some poetry. Actually, he'd give him great poetry, unheard of in this sunless place of despair. He recited aloud, gesturing with his right hand, his other hand at the button of his jacket:

> "*A fost odata ca-n povesti,*
> *A fost ca niciodata,*
> *Din rude mari împaratesti,*
> *O prea frumoasa fata.*"

"Georgiou's" jaw dropped and he let go of Ion's card. The gust of wind attempted to carry it, a lost butterfly with clipped wings, toward the sky the color of sour milk, but it was too heavy for a flight.

"Eminescu?" "Georgiou" said.

"The Bard's *Luceafârul*, The Evening Star," Ion said proudly. "The world-class literature as you say in America."

"Georgiou" took a dollar from the breast pocket of his shirt and handed it to Ion. "Take this as a nondeductible contribution to your worthy cause."

"Thank you," Ion said, taking the money. This donation would bring his grand total collection of the day to $1.89. He didn't feel thankful, of course, let alone understand what the man meant by "worthy cause." He made a mental note to look it up in the dictionary. Meanwhile, he stayed, hoping for some more funds.

"Listen, kinsman," "Georgiou" said. "We were practically neighbors. I used to live in the old Soviet Union, in Kishinev, a spit fly away from the Romanian border. They taught us Moldavian as a second language."

You are Russian, my wild friend, Ion thought. But I won't hold it against you.

"Moldavian is the younger brother to Romanian," he said aloud. He didn't believe half of the words the man was saying and didn't bother to understand the rest. All he knew was that the Russians took Kishinev from the Romanians, a crime long forgotten by the rest of humanity.

"How is Florica?" Ion had said to Doctor Virumi two days prior to meeting "Georgiou." Ion's stomach seemed strangely empty, as if a vital organ had been painlessly removed.

"She's asleep," Doctor Virumi had said.

The next day, riding in the subway next to Florica, her hand in his, Ion kept telling himself that Florica was out of danger, and as for the baby—it was a boy—he didn't care much about it. It wasn't a baby at all at this age anyway, he kept telling himself, knowing that it's a lie. The baby was the labor of love, his and Florica's, more than any poem in the world.

The hospital gave him a financial assistance form that he completed, and an administrator assured him that he would get 90% discount on services, and the other 10% he would have to pay in easy installments of $500 a month. Florica and he were home free thanks to the American health and judicial system.

But his boy was dead.

"Georgiou" stopped to read the card, unlike the vast majority of the locals. He spent too much time examining it, and even sniffed the card for some reason.

"*Romania Mare—nare ce mâncare,*" he said in broken Romanian, helped Ion to find his balance, and then switched to English. "You look like an intelligent, trustworthy man. You look like a poet. I need a favor from a foreign poet. You see, my bride is very romantic. A sucker for everything foreign. You help me, and I will give you another fifty of those."

"Another fifty dollars?" Ion said. Could a man wearing cotton pants be that rich?

"Yes, Mr. Bright. Another fifty dollars."

"What favor shall I perform for you?"

"I need you to go

with me and recite *Luceafârul* to my bride."

"A bride?" Ion said. "You want to do like one did in the past, hiring a troubadour singing a serenade to a lady? Are you serious?"

"That's the one, Mr. Troubadour," "Georgiou" said. "But you don't have to sing. Reciting would do just fine. By the way, my name is Vadim. Vah-dim. I'm Russian by birth and an American by necessity."

Vadim? Ion thought. It's not a name but a barbaric yawp.

"My name is Ion," he said aloud. "Not I-on. Not 'an atom or molecule in which the total number of electrons is not equal to the total number of protons', but 'gift of God' in Romanian. Ee-on… Is the lady a Romanian?"

"I know how to pronounce 'Ion.' I knew a guy by this name once. He wasn't a poet like you, but he was good with his tongue and his knife. No, the lady's not Romanian. She's as American as Saks Fifth Avenue and Jeep Cherokee Laredo."

Ion still didn't believe him. This was probably a trap and they would play him like a fiddle, but the smell of money was too irresistible. He followed "Georgiou," let him be "Vadim" if he so desired, to a flower store where the man bought a dozen roses. He was rich—he paid with a credit card—and that's why the flower girl treated him

Mark Budman

well. She even flirted with the man. Those Americans would do anything for money.

Then "Vadim" and Ion took a taxi to a part of the town Ion had never been to. They entered a restaurant more tastefully decorated than anything that Ion had seen in cosmopolitan Constanta. Staying next to her chair, Ion recited *Luceafârul* to a blonde woman in a white gown adorned with the rows of pearls, as beautiful as the earthly maiden the celestial being Luceafârul had descended to in the poem. She looked so young, and somehow Ion got a feeling she would never age.

Her jaw fell when he started reciting, and her cheeks turned to match her dress, but then she relaxed and smiled until the end. The patrons in the background returned to eating after the third stanza, and by the end of the fourth stanza the waiter was done picking up the broken plates, glass and food he had dropped—probably because of a temporary paralysis caused by awe—when Ion had started.

When Ion was done, he watched "Vadim" go down on one knee and propose to her. His ring was too narrow for Ion's taste, and probably only 14-carat gold, as it was common in America. When Ion had proposed, he gave his fiancé a 22-carat gold ring, though he had had to borrow an equivalent of $1000 American dollars—three-month salary—for it.

But the American woman accepted.

"Vadim" was right not to hire a guitarist or a

violinist—too trivial. Everyone hired a guitarist, violinist, or accordion player when they proposed. But to hire a poetry reciter was a splendid idea, in the best European tradition. Had the woman not accepted, Ion would have strangled her with his own hands.

He wiped his tears and went home with $51.89 in his pocket. He could buy Aurelia a new dress for that money.

But the most important thing was that he had just discovered that poetry wasn't dead after all if even the true, blue-blooded Americans were ready to part with a significant sum to listen to it. And if "Vadim" could make it in life, why couldn't Ion? What a Slav can do, so can a Romanian, only better.

Ion walked down the Fifth Avenue, lost in a thick crowd of total strangers, the natives of this strange land. But when he crossed the street, he felt the sun kissing his face, perhaps for the first time in America. He knew that the kiss would last only until he turned the corner, but still walked as fast as if the block stretched from here all the way to Constanta and then to the stars.

Visitation Rights

We live in a house divided. Between us and a neighbor. She is a witch and she has no kids. I know she ate them. She has big teeth and nose like a broken mushroom and she smells. She carries a broomstick. She flies at night and steals kids like me.

We have no running water. We pee and poop in an outhouse. I'm afraid the floor will break. And I'll fall into the hole. And the witch will laugh and say. What smells?

So I'm afraid to eat. If you don't eat, you don't poop. We don't have much to eat anyway. Just black bread, potatoes and onions. But we have a coo-coo clock. No one else has that.

There is an old man who's watching me. Not all the time. He looks like my Deda. Gray and wrinkled. And talks too much. He's dressed funny. With funny letters on his sweatshirt. They are not the right alphabet. He smiles at me. But I don't like him. He says he's me. He lies. He's old. And I'm a kid.

I tell mom. She says, I can't see the man. Is he your

imaginary friend? I say no. He's not my friend. He's not imaginary. He says to me, one day, you'll live in a different place. Lots of food to eat. No outhouse. He's a big fat liar. Everyone has an outhouse. Unless they are the Leaders.

A few years later, the man stopped coming.

I felt relieved when he was gone. He had become a distraction because I was busy preparing for college. When I was a kid, I refused to believe in distractions. The only distraction I believed in was the one that physically held my hands. While the visitor wasn't that type of distraction, he told me too many strange stories and got me confused.

I tried to forget him, and I succeeded.

Soon after that, I left the house, left the country, and planned to never come back. I built a new life, with a house with running water where I could poop in peace and safety. I bought a coo-coo clock like I had in my childhood.

As for the witches, I've never seen any flying over the neighborhood, though there was an abundance of broomsticks. As we all know, the lack of observation is not a proof of the negative.

If someone stole children around here, that usually was a divorced parent, who probably didn't eat them.

I got married, I got kids, I got grandkids.

I retired, my hair turned gray, I got wrinkles, and I began to look like Deda. And I bought a sweatshirt with

English letter (no wonder, it was an English-speaking country), and I built the time machine out of twelve broomsticks and the clockwork borrowed from a coo-coo clock. And then I remembered.

Doors

*Happiness is nothing more than good health
and a bad memory.*
—Albert Schweitzer

The leaves, wet and piled in layers, smother the deck
with the sticky smell of the forest floor. Muddy brown
and sickly yellow have replaced festive autumn colors.
The old man sweeps them off with a broom. His hands are
cold inside well-worn gloves. His joints—some are more
painful than others—creak over the patter of icy rain and
the howling of the wind.

He'd had trouble opening the door when he went from
the house to the deck. Rusty hinges, rusty lock, swollen
frame. Needs repairs, better yet, needs replacement. Who
has energy for that? His heart skips and sputters and
wheezes. What's that Chuck Norris joke? Ah... Chuck
Norris can never have a heart attack. His heart is too
chicken to attack him.

The old man fancies himself Hercules cleaning the

Augean stables, though Hercules probably did that in the summertime. And he was arthritis-free for sure.

Or maybe the futile struggle of the fisherman from *The Old Man and the Sea* is a more apt metaphor? The sea of leaves, right. The old man tries to think of a scientific reference, which is much closer to his field, but fails to come up with anything better than Brownian motion, which is technically not quite correct, because it's more random than futile.

You are three. There is a door in the front of your house, the threshold of which you are not allowed to cross. You are not a prisoner. You can go to the backyard through another door. The yard is all fenced in and overgrown with giant trees and bushes; it's dark there even on a sunny day. You are not alone. You can play with your cat Banditik, whose name means "robber" in the language of that land, and whose fur is the color of the late spring snow. You can draw figures on the tree bark with a crumbling piece of chalk, or pinch off the heads of bugs with your nails, or blow on the dandelions. You can lie on the grass and watch the leaves above you hugged by the breeze.

They are green and juicy and will stay this way forever. Unless you take them apart to examine them. You are a curious boy and get to the bottom of everything— ants, worms, leaves, the TV set—everything. You will be a doctor or scientist. A Nobel Prize winner.

Ten years ago, the old man was interviewed for TV, for yet another of his inventions. Was it *smellovision*—

the way to transmit smells over the Net—or just another enhanced fabrication of a silicon chip? He doesn't remember now. All his inventions are mashed together in his head like boiled potatoes under a fork.

The old man's interviewer, a girl in her twenties, asked him where he was from.

"The Soviet Union."

Her eyes, the color of amber, sparkled. "The Soviet Union? Was that the old name for Russia? The Evil Empire, right?"

He explained what the Soviet Union had been and how it was different from Russia. He told her about the origins of the Slavic people, about the Vikings, the Mongols, the Teutonic Knights, the czars, Lenin and Stalin, Sputnik, Gagarin, and about himself, the old man, being a relic of the Cold War washed up on American shores. She kept staring at him out of her ambers as if waiting for, like, the punch line of a joke.

Since he lost his job, he keeps telling this story to anyone willing to listen. Every year, the number of listeners gets fewer and fewer, even though the old man embellishes the story every time with new details: the girl was wearing a pendant in the shape of kissing doves; she had a boyfriend from Iran who got baptized against the wishes of his family to be with her; her cameraman was obese and he snored even when awake, plus he lusted after the girl but she treated him like a slave.

The old man even wrote an article about the interview

Mark Budman

for *The Resistor*, a semi-underground newspaper published by the trade-union wannabes; trade unions were not allowed at his company. They promised to publish it, but they never did.

The front door is what attracts you. You see exceedingly bright light and hear music every time the door opens. You see tall figures, aglow. You have already tried to sneak out, but one member or the other of your family has always stopped you. They kiss and hug you, but you bite, kick, and shriek every time. You could complain that they take away your personal freedoms, but you can't express yourself well yet.

You ask, "What's in there?"

"Eternal life," they say.

"What's eternal?"

"It lasts forever."

"What's forever?"

Your family is on the move one rainy night, and your father carries you, all wrapped up in his raincoat, while you are sleeping. Dogs growl a block away, motors run, and sharp commands shatter the silence to splinters.

Your family escapes the town, the country, the continent in a hurry, leaving everything behind but you. You never have a chance to see what was outside that door. When you grow up, you want to go back. It's safe for you now, but it's too far, you've forgotten the language, it's expensive, and you are always busy.

One day, when you are old and stooped and get a

backache from lying on the grass, you will go to bed and wake up in your old house again. You'll get up, get dressed in your best clothes, and walk without a cane. You'll come to the front door. No one will stop you now. You'll be turning the knob. You'll be pushing. You'll be crossing the threshold.

Now, only a few dozen leaves remain on the deck. A worm wiggles obscenely among them. In fact, they are so few that the old man can count each leaf before it's gone. One for each member of the family who left him one way or another. One for each friend he's lost. One for each of his golden years past. One for each of the lovers he can hardly remember.

The last leaf is stuck and the old man can't dislodge it with the broom or his shoe. He takes off his right glove and bends over to remove the leaf with his cold, stiff fingers. Now, only the worm remains on the icy-smooth surface of the deck. The man leans on his broom.

"What's your name, Sir?" he asks the worm. "Do you have children? Any friends? A wife, perhaps? Are you on Medicare? The premiums are stingy, aren't they? Have you ever read Nabokov? You know that he shared the same first name and the patronymics as Putin, that snake—Vladimir Vladimirovich? Isn't that a shame? Do you approve of Obamacare? I mean, no preconditions is good, but the cost aspects of it concern me... And terrorism.... It's a shame that people are not afraid to blow up themselves for a false idea... I'll tell you, when some years ago I was interviewed for TV..."

The cold water seeps through his torn boots. The old man wants to return to the marginal warmth of his house and to close the door behind him. The worm will wait. Its patience is legendary. And it can smell. Such an endearing creature.

But the door gets stuck again. He's trying to turn the knob. He's pushing. He must cross the threshold. But the door doesn't budge. He knows that the front door is locked from the inside. There is no way back to the house. His heart flickers like a dying ember. He staggers. He falls. He floats. He hears music, and turns toward the suddenly bright light and sees tall figures, aglow. They salute him. He salutes back.

He hears the door opening behind him with a groan, shallow like the first breath.

Her Time Pieces

Perhaps the girl wasn't born inside the hourglass.
Perhaps someone put her there in the months following
her birth. She's heard a story—perhaps it was a fairy
tale—that her mother came from a faraway land and
spoke the language of birds.

She wasn't sure where she came from and didn't
care. She didn't remember her mother, but only the sharp
caress of the sand grains on her skin and the strange,
mysterious world, dark and brooding, outside the glass.
But the world wasn't too big. Later, she learned that the
hourglass was stored inside a cupboard.

By the age of five or so—it was hard to measure time
when no one flipped the hourglass—she got transferred
into a mechanical pocket watch. That was awful: hot and
cramped and nothing to see but cogs, mindless in their
workaholic fashion. Fortunately, it didn't last long. In a
few weeks, the girl ended up in a coo-coo clock. Such
a relief. Plenty of space, and the coo-coo didn't bother
the girl, but just told her stories of the outside world it

Mark Budman

observed when announcing the time. The girl loved to hear about the great room in which they lived, lovely picture windows, a square below the windows and a clock tower across with a giant clock that chimed in a solid, confident voice. But she especially liked the stories about the forest in which the coo-coo said it grew before being caught and imprisoned in the clock. The coo-coo told about strange and vicious beasts, squirrels, sparrows, and rabbits, and about the magical *Alenky* flower that could turn wood, stone, and metal into a living being.

By the age of eighteen, the girl met a boy who lived in the clock tower across the square.

That happened one morning, when he knocked at her clock. She had never seen a man her size up close. Or any human being that small, or that handsome. And he had wings. Even the coo-coo bird had no wings.

"You are lovely," he said. "You are lovelier than my iPhone." She didn't know what an iPhone was, but she enjoyed the sound of his voice. And she blushed.

"My name is Josh. What is your name, pretty lady?"

She curtsied.

She climbed on his back and he flew her to his tower. She saw a lot of moving hats below, and some great beasts Josh called 'cars.'

"Promise never to walk across the square," he said. "Or the pedestrians would crush you underfoot and the cars run you over."

She didn't know what 'pedestrians' were and what,

if any, they had to do with the moving hats, but promised anyway.

He showed her his room, his iPhone, and a closet full of wings of every color. The iPhone looked like a giant mirror, much taller than the girl, but it had pictures in it.

On their wedding night, Josh leaned out to the street and shouted, "I love my wife." The girl blushed.

He turned around and was hit on the head by the pendulum. "If writing in all caps means shouting, then all lower-case letters are whispering," he said before expiring. "I love you. The password to the iPhone is tattooed on the palm of my hand."

The girl decided she had to revive him. She had to find the magical *Alenky* flower. She attached Josh's wings, but had no idea how to fly. She climbed down the tower wall, crossed the square at night, lest be run over by cars or crushed underfoot by the mysterious pedestrians. She climbed up the wall again and ended up in her old coo-coo clock.

"Take me to the forest," she said to the bird. "I need the magical *Alenky* flower to revive my husband."

"But I have no wings," the coo-coo said. "I can't fly."

It had no mouth or eyes, but it omitted those details.

"Try this pair," the girl said.

The coo-coo attached the wings and flew over the room.

"Yehoo!" it cried.

Then it landed back and said in a bored voice, "They

will do."

"Can we go to the forest now?"

The coo-coo looked away. "Um."

"What's the matter?"

"I don't know how to put this to you... There is no magical *Alenky* flower. That is to say, maybe there is; maybe there is not."

"What do you mean?" The girl frowned.

The coo-coo's face turned red, or so it seemed. "Frankly, my dear, I made up the magical *Alenky* flower. As for squirrels, sparrows, and rabbits, they may or may not be vicious. I've never even been to the forest. I've spent all my life inside this darn clock."

The girl sat on the floor and cried. The coo-coo embraced her with its wings.

"There is a way," it finally said. "I've heard of this magician Siri who lives inside the iPhone. If you say, 'Hey Siri, what's the best sushi place in town?' the magician tells you. Whatever 'sushi' means."

The girl jumped up. "Did you say iPhone?"

The coo-coo flew the girl across the square.

Josh was still there on the floor, still dead. The girl took his cold hand. The words "Whisky, Bravo, Tango" were tattooed on his palm. That had to be either the names of his previous loves or his password.

She entered the words into the iPhone, and it lit up. She said, "Siri, how do I revive my husband?"

She expected a fairy to appear, with wings and white

flowing dress and a magic wand, but instead an inhuman but pleasant voice said, "Call 911. I can dial it for you."

The ambulance came. They took Josh to the hospital and the doctors attached a new head to him. So he became even more handsome than before.

The couple opened a watch factory in Vietnam, and marketed them under the brand name "Watch Your Love." They put the coo-coo in charge of manufacturing because it could wing anything, and Siri in charge of marketing. The watches were a great commercial success, sold for $19.99 at Wal Mart and on Amazon. The couple had two twin girls and two boys they named Eeny, Meeny, Miny, and Moe, who were very fond of sushi when they grew up. The couple lived happily ever after, but the mother spent a lot of her precious free time staring at an hourglass, a timeless smile on her still-beautiful face. In fact so beautiful that Josh began to suspect that she would never age.

Love and Faith
in the Shadow of Lenin

Ye Gods! Annihilate but space and time/
And make two lovers happy.
—Alexander Pope

In the sixth grade, Nikifor Vladimirovich Rosanov
sat behind Praskovia Nikitichna Tarasova in every class
and pulled her pigtails. She had such luxurious hair—
even silkier and thicker than his Siberian cat—and her
nails were trimmed, unlike the cat's.

Praskovia shrieked and Nikifor grinned. She slapped
him and he laughed. She threw books and pens and apple
cores at him and he caught them in the air. She helped
him with math, and he helped her with Russian, especially
with poetry.

He walked her home—they lived in the Butovo
suburb of Moscow—and she kicked any girl who so much
as batted her eyelashes at him.

At the time, the Soviet Union looked almost

healthy to an outsider. Gorbachev was only considering perestroika, Yeltsin drunk his vodka in Sverdlovsk, and Putin was a lowly KGB officer.

Nikifor and Praskovia first had sex at sixteen. Nikifor began the wooing attack with "Your cheeks are like roses."

Perhaps reading in her eyes that the line wasn't poetic enough, he quickly quoted his favorite poet, Mayakovsky:

"*The world is again in flowers like in hairs/the world again is a visage of spring.*"

The year before, when he'd saved enough dough, Nikifor had tattooed Mayakovsky's "*Lenin and the Party are twins and brothers*" on his arm. He told Praskovia later that he was impressed by the sheer logic of this quote—twins were not necessarily brothers. The tattoo had become infected, and he'd ended up with indelible red-and-blue blotches resembling the American election map.

Now, softened by the "visage of spring" ekphrasis and by the close proximity to the map, Praskovia's defenses melted completely.

Afterwards, they lay on his raincoat in the cranberry bushes. Cold rain pelted their partially naked bodies. The event happened on a collective farm where the whole class was sent to harvest potatoes. The colors around them were brown, black, and grey. So the bit of red between Praskovia's thighs was a welcome splash of color.

But several years into the marriage, one evening after

lovemaking, Nikifor told her that she had gained too much weight. You're like a woman from a museum painting, he said. Rubens, he said. Unless it was Rubin. She vaguely remembered hearing this Jewish name before. He painted flying cows, didn't he?

She knew Nikifor was right. She had gained at least two kilos after the marriage. Maybe three. But he shouldn't have said that. Truth could have been the best defense, but it still was an offense. He pushed her off her pedestal. He was comparing her to a cow.

He was an important man now—a janitor at Lenin's Mausoleum—the job he acquired partially on merit, thanks to his skills with the broom, the dusting cloth, and the imported Spic and Span, and partially due to his networking connections—he was the drinking buddy of the Janitor-in-Chief. Soon, his buddy was fired after being caught stealing Spic and Span, and Nikifor was promoted to Chief.

Perhaps, in his mind, this important position gave him the right to look down at his wife, a plain grocery store cashier.

Nikifor's comment put Praskovia in a state of perpetual shock. From that point on, she undressed only to take a shower, and only when no one else was home. Even then, she closed her eyes while washing herself. If she peeked by mistake, her face reddened and her breath quickened, and she'd make the water cold. That would serve her right.

She made love to her husband in a nightshirt, and no matter how much he begged, it stayed on.

And then the nightmares came. Her sleep had become like a free fall into an abyss. Foul winged creatures with long beaks, fiery eyes, and devastatingly large bellies circled around her, assaulting her ears with their rambling cries. She fought for breath, but the pressure on her chest was too heavy and her struggle to awaken lasted until dawn.

One night, after downing half a glass of her husband's vodka, she had a different dream. A man in a white, floor length gown, sandals, and a crown of thorns pulled her out of the abyss by her thick, brown, slightly grey-streaked hair, and called softly, "Praskovia, Praskovia." He resembled David Stein, her upstairs neighbor—curly black hair, longish nose, and sad, dove-like eyes.

Then she noticed another man, red-skinned, barrel-chested, furry-legged, two-horned, with a lump of smoldering coal, shaped like a cigarette, in his hand.

Praskovia awoke, coughing, wiping her tears with her large fists, suitable for a middleweight boxer, and shaking sizable breasts barely covered by a torn flannel nightshirt. Her cigarette, which she'd forgotten to extinguish before falling asleep, had made a hole in her pillow, and smoke was filling the tiny bedroom. Nikifor slept next to her, snoring like a creature from hell.

The next day, Praskovia visited her aunt Pasha, a nursing aid at the woman's hospital.

Mark Budman

"It was the Savior," Pasha said, pursing her thin, pale lips. "Him for sure. He saved you because He wants you."

Pasha was always nagging her to join the Nephews and Nieces of the Savior, a branch of an American sect that had made big waves in Moscow in the last several years. Pasha herself had been a Niece in good standing for close to a year and claimed she'd never felt better.

"I even lost two kilos," she said one day. "It's like ice cream for the soul," she said the next. "I feel like my head is already in heaven," she said the following week.

"I'll think about it," Praskovia gave her usual reply, but in the back of her mind she felt the mighty pull of the new religion.

Three days after the dream, Praskovia immersed herself in a barrel of lukewarm water and was pronounced a Niece by Shepherd Golovin who looked like a cartoon Biblical prophet from a Communist-era anti-religion poster. He was equipped with a flying gray beard, tangled hair full of dandruff, a dirty white gown, a heavy crucifix hanging from a thin neck, penetrating mad eyes, and a wooden staff that was so crudely made that it must have left splinters in his hand.

A month after Praskovia was born again, when she was still a bit shaky on her feet, her grocery store manager, Vladimir Pisulin, caught her in a dark closet and grabbed her breasts through her uniform. He was squat like a barrel of pickles, and he smelled of Lysol and tobacco as always, but she had quit smoking now, and she found the resulting smell repulsive. Praskovia pushed him away with all her considerable might. He hit his head on the opposite wall and landed on his bottom, which was twice the size of a standard toilet seat.

"You're fired, bitch," he cried, trying unsuccessfully to rise to his feet. "Fired!"

Praskovia came home, fell on her knees, and spoke in tongues. She'd seen other Nieces and Nephews do it many times, but she had always failed until now.

Nikifor returned from work early that day. His face was unusually white and forlorn. The smell of beer preceded him by what the telephone company would have considered a long distance.

Praskovia met him at the door and before he opened his mouth, she told him in Pushtu, "They fired me."

"Huh?" Nikifor said. As far as Praskovia knew, he spoke only Russian.

"They fired me," Praskovia continued in the language he understood. "Because I'm a Niece of the Savior."

"Why can't you be an Orthodox?" Nikifor sat down. "Or a Catholic? Or a Muslim? Or Jewish? Or even an atheist like me? They would leave you alone if you were like the rest of us. No, you have to be different!

"They're going to fire me, too," he added after a moment.

Praskovia uttered a wail, got to her feet, and walked closer to her husband. "What for?"

"Because they're going to close the Mausoleum and bury Lenin. No one needs him anymore. No one but me."

"No way."

He sighed. "Say what you want. He'll be gone, and I'll be fired."

She rubbed her forehead, stimulating the thinking process. "Let's immigrate to America," she said. "It's the land of religious freedom. That's for sure."

Nikifor fixed her with a heavy stare. "Are you sure, Praskovia? To exchange the land of Mayakovsky for the land of hip-hop? To be rich instead of poor? To travel the world instead of taking the Metro to Sokolniki Park on Sunday afternoons? To be on welfare instead of working daily? Is that the life you want for you and me?"

"Yes, I'm sure. All people make sacrifices. Even the Savior died on the cross."

"But the American government won't let us in. They have Homeland Security now. It's like our old KGB, but instead of preventing people from leaving, they prevent people from getting in."

"We'll tell them we were both persecuted on account of my religion."

Nikifor grinned. "Yes, Praskovia. That might work. We are moving to America. We'll apply for the visa tomorrow."

Praskovia gasped. She expected stiff opposition, and now she hesitated. Things that progressed too easily were suspicious. This rollercoaster was going a bit too fast for her even though it was she who'd ordered the ride. She went to their bedroom, closed the door, fell on her knees, and began to pray. Soon, she was talking in tongues again. Then the man who looked like David Stein appeared on a white cloud. He was stooping lest he strike his head against the ceiling.

"Should I move to America, Savior?" she asked in Swahili. "My husband wants me to. And you said I have to obey him."

He put his hand on her head. It felt warm and reassuring. "America is not what it used to be. The spawn of the anti-Savior is raising its ugly head there," he answered in Hebrew. "So they need you now. Go."

She opened her eyes, and she saw herself in an American church, among warriors of the Savior, next to a tall, blond American pastor—no beer belly or tobacco smoke here. The church's doors were barricaded with pews. The spawn of the Enemy came as the clock struck twelve, bursting through the door as if it were wet paper and scattering heavy pews as if they were Lincoln logs.

Praskovia held the Book of the Apostle Bud the Unworthy with both hands above her head. She saw one of the spawn, a man in a pink suit and a green shirt, with an earring in his left ear, fangs bared, jumping at the pastor. The monster's roar reverberated in her ears. She was about to run to the pastor's defense, but a woman in a blue surgical gown armed with a dilator and curette

Mark Budman

breathed fire in her face. Praskovia dodged and hit the creature across the muzzle with the Book. The demon fell to the floor and disintegrated. Praskovia, shaking, sweaty, looked around. The warriors stood their ground, their weapons at the ready. The spawn was gone and everyone burst into a hymn.

"Go, child, and serve me well," David Stein said. "The victory will be ours."

A few minutes later, Praskovia came out to her husband. Her eyes shone and her cheeks were aflame. He watched her, his mouth agape. She took him by the hand.

"So, will you go with me?" he asked in a trembling voice.

"I will go where you go. Your people will be my people. Your country will be my country."

He exhaled. His voice was steady now. "And your ass will be mine," he said and pulled her by the hand toward the bedroom.

Under his familiar weight, she closed her eyes and prepared to grit her teeth. Yet a strange new sensation jolted her body into another plane of existence. She opened her eyes and saw a kind face next to her. It was Nikifor, yet his features were strangely fluid, changing into David Stein's and back. Hope entered Praskovia like a caress of passion. The nightmare was about to go away. She was open for a miracle now. America awaited her, and miracles happen in America. She would assert her womanly rights. She should've done that a long time ago. Freedom, equality and female power. Fuck the patriarchy.

She slid away from under Nikifor and took her slip off.

Super Couple

Soupmann is Superman's third cousin twice removed.
Unlike his relative, Soupmann set his priorities logically
and succinctly. He fights for truth and justice, and
sometimes for truth and the American way, and sometimes
for justice and the American way, but not for all three at
once. Otherwise, he'd be stretching too thin. He goes into
a phone booth and turns into chicken soup. He smothers
the bad guys and nourishes the victims. Despite the soup
being chicken, Soupmann is not Jewish. He has two Ns
at the end of his name. He's not even human. He's out
of this world. He is an immigrant from Kryptonian, and
the soup is fluorescent-green. 10% kryptonite and 90%
secret ingredients. No one knows how it tastes, because
whoever tasted it is either dead or turned mum with awe.

Soupmann meets Saltwoman at a Superman's party for
super-weirdos. She is Superman's second cousin thrice
removed, also an immigrant. She goes into a phone booth
and turns into kosher salt because she is kind of Jewish,

in a very reformed, Kryptonian way. Also, the kosher salt's properties make it easier to sprinkle it on bad guys. She raises their blood pressure. She is dangerous in high doses, but zesty in small. Her parents thought she was salt of the earth, er, of Krypton.

They first meet when he is in his soup form. She falls all over him in her salt form. They fall in love. It's zesty. They get married. Superman and Spiderman are guests of honor. A rabbi and a priest officiate. After the ceremony, they walk into a full bar. Spiderman accidentally pushes Superman, who spills some soup on his cape. Soupmann rubs salt into the wound by telling a Superman joke. Why is Superman's shirt so tight? Because he's wearing a size S. Superman glares at him. Soupmann boils. He's not sure if mere 10% kryptonite can hurt Superman. The guests panic. They expect super trouble. They know that the bystanders get hurt in this case while the superheroes always survive. Saltwoman gets between Superman and Soupmann and says, "Let's not fight at my wedding. Come on, Superman, let's dance instead." Everyone is happy, especially the guests who thought they would never get out alive.

Soupmann and Saltwoman coordinate their efforts. The bad guys are unhappy. They panic. They scream and pull out copious amounts of their own and bystanders' hair. They consider quitting their trade and going into politics.

Mark Budman

But one of them invents cell phones. The invention goes viral. Everyone gets the cells now. The phone booths quickly disappear. Soupmann and Saltwoman can't find a place to turn. Without turning, they can't fight the crime. Soupmann turns sour. Saltwoman crumbles. They panic.

Saltwoman spends her days spilled all over the carpet. It's a bad omen. She is a mess. Soupmann soaks in the tub or, rather, soaks the tub. He pockmarks the enamel. The bad guys are happy. They chat on the cell phones, telling Soupmann and Saltwoman jokes. Saltwoman is a salt with a deadly weapon. Hah-hah-hah. What's so special about Twitter alphabet soup? It has only 140 letters. Hah-hah-hah. They post on Facebook and they tweet. They give each other likes.

Soupmann has a Eureka moment. He comes out of the bathroom, dripping. He's lost weight and is all bones. "Forget the phone booth. We should go to a Wal-Mart and turn there," he says. "No one pays any attention to anyone at Wal-Mart. It's full of weirdos, and it's open 24/7." Saltwoman pulls herself together.

They turn successfully in a Wal-Mart. No one pays attention to them, though one associate makes a half-assed attempt to mop them. They resume their fight again. The bad guys are unhappy. They panic. They form a secret group on Facebook and give each other 'sad' emoticons.

Soupmann meets Goyawoman in the International Food aisle of Wal-Mart. She's a spicy beauty with a green card. They are having a one-night stand on the empty shelf every night. Saltwoman catches burritos on Soupmann's breath. Soupmann confesses. Saltwoman files for divorce. The bad guys are happy.

Goyawoman has no powers except for her beauty, ability to speak 100 words a minute, and cooking skills. Soupmann gets bored. He goes back to Saltwoman and asks for forgiveness on his knees. Saltwoman tells him she is pregnant with twins. She takes him back. They fight the bad guys together again. Meanwhile, Goyawoman meets Ramenman. They fall in love. They open a restaurant "Spicy, Tasty, Confused." Perhaps they meant "conflated." Everyone is happy except for the bad guys. They go through so many cycles of being happy and unhappy that they can't stand it anymore. The politics are saturated. No new politicians are needed. So the bad guys reform and join the law enforcement.

Saltwoman gives birth to a boy and a girl. They have powers right in the crib. The boy can crawl up the wall and projectile-vomit through steel plates, and the girl can double the level of lead in Chinese-made pacifiers to 100%. Saltwoman can't sleep. What if her kids won't find the bad guys to fight? They would be bored. There is nothing worse than bored superkids. Saltwoman panics. She's ready to fall apart. Soupmann assures her that the kids' future is bright. New bad guys are born every day. So, the kids won't be bored for long. Saltwoman is happy. Soupmann and she make love. It's even tastier than before, taken with a pinch of salt.

Rezoning Nazis Drink Alphabet Soup

The skinheads will drive down our streets, he says, thirteen of them to a flat-bed truck. The trucks will be painted with the Confederate flag and swastikas. The skinheads will throw empty beer bottles and cans and shout Nazi slogans. Maybe they will even fire-bomb houses.

They are not skinheads, I say. They are students.

Michael is staring at me as if I just said that global warming has been cancelled for the next millennium. I stare back. I love pissing contests.

No, he finally says. It doesn't matter if they know what the integral is or who wrote Shakespeare's plays. They act like skinheads. That's what counts.

OK, I say. I'll sign your petition.

We turn to Arkady.

What, he says.

Will you sign a petition against the skinhead housing to be built on our street, Michael says.

No way, he says. I'm apolitical. I don't believe in petitions, voting or global warming.

Michael, Arkady, and I are househusbands. Scratch that. Scratch that with a marking pen, or, better yet, with a knife. We are kept men, though we are neither young nor handsome. We are not even athletic anymore. Our respected wives keep us mostly out of habit and an exaggerated sense of duty. To give them additional credit, they don't keep us in damp cellars, rat-infested towers, or in cupboards under the stairs, but in their spare bedrooms, or, sometimes, even in their own bedrooms, in their own beds. We aren't locked up all day or forced to wear transparent silk pajamas. At first glance, we look like normal albeit aging men. But, like wives of centuries past, we don't work, and are totally dependent on the generosity of our spouses. We used to work, but we lost our jobs to younger men with newer, shinier diplomas, polished social skills, and up-to-date clothing.

I call us the Three Stooges. Michael and Arkady hate when I do this, so I don't do it often.

On this Monday morning, dreadful to the people who have to go to work, the three of us assemble in Arkady's wife's house. We sit in the spare bedroom where he usually sleeps unless his wife calls him for conjugal duties, which she doesn't do anymore.

Arkady was an engineer, but now is a photographer, specializing in nudes. When I first met him, I asked if he does nude men or nude animals. I said that my wife calls me a tom cat, which is an animal. Arkady gave me his sharp photographer's look as if calculating the right f-stop and exposure, and said in his funny Russian accent that he does only nude women between ages 18 and 30. I said that I'm out of the question as his model, and he agreed. Arkady sells his photographs in an online gallery and invests the resulting money in photo gear. Last year, he made enough to buy a polarizing filter and a new bag. Arkady's overweight and resembles the letter D.

Michael was a programmer, but now is a handyman. If your washing machine hose is busted or you need to prune your shrubs, Michael is your man. He invests the money he makes in sunglasses, designer shirts, and cigarettes. Last year, he made enough to buy imitation Ralph Lauren glasses, an Old Navy shirt, and a carton of Ace cigarettes.

He's wide-shouldered and resembles the letter V.

He is also a community activist. Last year he protested against a new Walmart. The year before it was a water treatment plant. And the other day he bought what he claimed to be an antique statuette of Venus. His wife doesn't know about it yet.

I always sign his petitions. None of them has worked yet.

I was a lawyer, but now I'm a writer. If you need legal advice, especially if you broke your leg or your dog bit the postman, go somewhere else. I invest the money I make on writing in computers. Last year, I made enough

Mark Budman

to buy a new wireless keyboard.

I don't know what I resemble. I guess it's the letter I because I like to talk about myself.

My favorite subject is my book. Its subject is me. Its history is not a rollercoaster, because rollercoasters are cliché, and a writer who uses clichés ought to be pelted unconscious with crumpled rejection letters. I tell anyone who is willing to listen about my book's ups and downs. I tell about the six New York City agents who competed for the right to represent it. I settled with one who wooed me the most. She kept calling me every day and she was sweeter than molasses. She said that I needed some minor edits, though. Nothing wrong with the edits, right? That's what agents are for. To woo the writer and to request edits. We made an agreement that she would send the manuscript out to the publishers in the beginning of the year even if she didn't like my edits. But then she turned around and told me that I'm lazy and that she's not willing to continue our relationship.

"But we had an agreement," I said, gripping the phone so hard that I was about to squeeze water out of it.

"Let's not get into he said, she said," she said.

So I found another agent. Everyone I know has heard this story. Several times.

Nobody talks for a while. The silence is oppressive, like the moment before a thunderstorm. Michael takes out a cigarette, but Arkady waves him to quit.

Our wives are like punctuation marks. My wife is

an exclamation point because she walks very erect and tolerates no dissent. Arkady's wife is a question mark because she's slightly stooped and she always questions authority. Michael's wife is a period because she is small, and when she makes a statement, there is no way to continue the conversation.

I wonder how Arkady and Michael see them. Maybe as a collection of lenses and flashes, or drill bits and hammers.

"My wife kicked me out," Michael says. "Together with my Venus. I've been staying at a motel for three days. They're partying in the next room non-stop. Can I stay with one of you for a while?"

Now, it's Arkady and me who exchange glances. Michael's wife's name is Shulamite. There are several ways to pronounce it, and she favors one of them, naturally. I always get it mixed up for some reason so I never say her name.

"Please," Michael says. "I'm broke."

"Sure," I say, though I'm far from being sure. After all, I'm not the man of the house. Worse yet, I'm so intensely private that I'm ashamed of my own house mirrors. What if he would parade naked in front of me? But he's my friend, and any one of us could be in his shoes. I have no choice.

"As long as you're not going to smoke," I say. "But what happened?"

"I wish I knew," Michael says. "All she told me was

enough is enough."

"That's not very telling," Arkady says.

An hour later, I drag one of Michael's suitcases into the spare bedroom. It's gray with blue stripes, the color of his mood. He drags another two behind me. I don't know how I will break the news to my wife when she comes home. Will she also kick me out?

We store the suitcases in the corner, careful not to touch the freshly painted walls. I bring out the sheets, pillow and blanket for the cot, and a towel. I show him the bathroom. He sits on the cot and I sit in the chair. He's so bent over that he resembles the letter S now. His face is blank. So is probably mine. We are the mirror reflection of each other, though this is a warped mirror. We are ready for my wife's arrival. I'm sure she will start with an exclamation point. I'm afraid of her, but she doesn't know that. I'm good at hiding my emotions. That's what both Michael and Arkady say.

"Will you go to the town council meeting with me tomorrow?" Michael asks.

I went last year. The aisle was full of older people. Some sat on the floor. Michael made a speech about the quality of life being compromised by Walmart. The councilmen counted their fingernails. An old woman coughed next to me. She tried to stop, but failed. Her eyes were about to pop out of their orbits. I grinned at Michael and flashed him victory signs.

"Sure," I say. "We will overcome."

When my wife comes home, she's so tired that she hardly says a word. She's ready for some Zs. She only asks the most important questions: "How's Shulamite? Do the kids know?" I know she says "Shulamite" right because Michael's wife never corrects her. On the other hand, maybe Shulamite is afraid of my wife. A female soul is always a mystery.

Then my wife gets on her tippy-toes and kisses me on the cheek. "Don't be afraid," she says. "I love you."

She told me recently that I'm gliding on the surface of life like a water bug, nonchalant and unattached. I wanted to say like Jesus, but she doesn't appreciate my jokes anymore.

She retires to the master bedroom. I whisper, "I love you, too. More than ever." I hope she knows. After all, she keeps me here for some reason that probably goes beyond nostalgia and habit. We share more than just children. Common beliefs and experiences may sound not as glamorous as passion and love at first sight, but they make a great foundation even for an air castle. So what if Eros doesn't shoot at us anymore? Who needs the brat? We read the same books, squeeze the toothpaste from the top, pray the same way, love Rome and hate Paris, and never salt our food. We always did things our way and if someone doesn't like it, let him suck the dead bull's dick, as Arkady says.

I close the door to Michael's room. I brush my teeth and get ready for bed, a different one from my wife's. In the mirror, a pissing man resembles the letter Q.

Usually, I fall asleep pretty fast, especially now that my wife bought me a daybed to replace the aging sofa, but tonight I watch the super-bright digits of my alarm clock as if I've never seen them before. I'm not used to a third person in the house. The kids don't show up here often.

I hear Michael tip-toeing to the bathroom. No matter how he tries, I hear every sound, culminating into the loud explosion of a flushing toilet.

I haven't had to count sheep for years, ever since about a month after my forceful retirement, but I think that old habits die hard. Indeed, when I begin to count, it comes as natural as the blinking of an eye.

I fall asleep after the clock signals 2 AM. I dreamed of skinheads lined up by the trucks. Each has an egg-shaped head. Their trucks are adorned with a slogan: "Say *Yes* to re-zoning." Our wives are feeding them alphabet soup. Then came Michael and began to crack the boys' heads at the edge of a flat-bed truck.

At 10 in the morning, Michael and I are having breakfast. My wife is long gone to work. I serve cereal with low fat milk in glass bowls and boiled eggs with whole wheat toasts. No one promised Michael gourmet cooking, but this food is healthy. He asks for the salt. I scramble to find it. We don't salt anything in our house.

I watch in horror how he salts his eggs. Arkady says that testicles and eggs are the same word in Russian. He's nuts. He likes the alphabet soup. He said they didn't have that in Russia. Even if they did, it would have been a different alphabet. Do Cyrillic letters taste different? I bet you it would be difficult to make such two-part letters as "ы" and "й."

"What?" Michael says, intercepting my gaze.

I open my mouth to lecture him on the dangers of salt, but tell him about my book instead.

"My newest agent is too slow," I say. "He's never met a deadline yet."

"Really?" he says.

"*Really* means that you don't believe me."

"No. It only means that I'm listening emphatically."

"So what do you think I should do?" I ask.

"About what?"

"About my newest agent?"

Michael cracks open another egg. I guess it's his third. Too much cholesterol.

"Fire him," he says.

"He's a volunteer firefighter," I say. "How can I fire a fireman?"

I have no idea if it's true. This just came to my mind, and there it was, I said it without a second thought. I can't fire an unresponsive agent even if he isn't a fireman, of course. He'd be hurt. How can I fire anyone? They can fire me, and they did, but that doesn't mean I can treat someone else the same shitty way.

"He has already sent my novel out," I say. "I'll give him a grace period."

"Like a credit card company?"

"Something like that. If he doesn't act, I'll turn him over to a collection agency."

Michael salts his third egg. I've seen him eating before, but it was never like this. Now I know why he's overweight. I can't stand it any longer. I get up and wash my dishes. Will he wash his, or does he expect I should serve him? He washes his. Still, the wave of irritation hits the walls of my stomach.

I let him watch TV while I get on my computer. It's supposed to be my writing time, but I waste the first hour on chats with wannabe writers. After all, I don't need to punch a clock anymore. I never did, but now I don't have to do it even figuratively speaking.

The phone rings. It has to be my wife. She is checking on me daily. She worries about my health. It's actually my agent. He tells me that he sold my novel.

I don't know what to say. It's so totally unexpected, like $1.50 a gallon gasoline at the pump, or a young beautiful woman winking at me in the street. Shouldn't there be some rejections first? The publishers always send rejections. That's what they do for a living. Anything else is a breach of trust.

"Really?" I say.

I know that he's aggressive and is much younger than me, but have no idea what he looks like. He's probably like that sign on the key above the period. A forward flying arrow tip. I like him.

"*Really* means that you don't believe me."

"No. It only means that I'm listening emphatically."

He pauses as if trying to parse my remark. Good luck. I would fail as well if I were him.

"It's a so-called preemptive bid," he says. "They paid more to assure the deal. Congratulations, sir. It's a good start for your career. The check is coming. I'll be in touch more."

I feel empty like after sex but without the elation. For the last several years I had a goal—to publish my book. Now that I'm goal-less, what's next? I'm a bullet without a target. I'm adrenaline without blood vessels. I'm a mosquito without the sense of smell.

The phone rings again. It's Shulamite. She doesn't want me because who am I? Just an empty sound, a few random letters. She wants Michael. She sounds like she really wants him, and she wants him now. I call him to the phone, and as soon as he picks up his, I hang up, resisting the writer's temptation to listen in.

Ten minutes later, Michael knocks at my door. His hair sticks in all directions and his eyes dart back and forth. He leans against the frame and says, "I told Shulamite that I donated my Venus to charity. Funny, I didn't even lie. Now, Shulamite wants me back."

"That's good, isn't it?" I say. That's actually excellent. She will take him back and I won't need to see him salting his eggs. That's what they call win-win and I call winning a lottery.

Mark Budman

"I don't know if it's good," he says. "I like it here."

"We like to have you." Right. If you lay off the eggs and the salt.

"I think I should go, though. She sounds sincere."

"Well, if she sounds sincere, maybe you're right. It's good to make peace with sincere women."

"You're pulling my leg," he says.

"No, I'm sincere."

I help him drag his suitcases to his car. A birdy pooped on its hood. In some cultures, it's a good sign.

"I hope she won't change her mind," he says and lights a cigarette. His hands shake.

"She won't," I say. "By the way, my agent just sold my book. Isn't that funny or what?"

"How do you know she won't change her mind? She has before."

I don't know what to say. Did I lower my voice too much when I delivered the good news? When I call Arkady, I'll be as loud as a thunderbolt. I'll make sure he hears me clearly as if I were talking to an idiot.

"Because she's a good woman," I finally say, closing the trunk. We slap each other on the shoulders. We shake each other's hand. We look each other square in the eyes. That's what men do.

We used to support each other either by sword, bows and arrows and spear, back in the time when we hunted mammoths while women tended the fire and cooked soup. Too bad they don't cook soup anymore. I would take anything, even alphabet soup would do, though I prefer Russian borscht, but they don't have time and we never learned how.

Even worse is that the fire has long been gone. We all missed its sparks and warmth, and that delicious, bitter smoke that filled your lungs to the fullest, reminding you that you were still alive.

I can hear the skinheads revving up their engines down the street. If I ask Michael, each of them carries a rifle with an attached bayonet in his outstretched hand, forming a letter H. Michael would say H is for hate. Humor me, Michael.

I'd rather see the letter E everywhere. E for eternity. I grin.

Mark Budman

Five Minutes after Midnight

American Zolushka is half-asleep in his arms, dressed in an ash-colored slip under an ash-covered blanket and ash-colored sheets. Make it three-quarters asleep. Before they met, she hardly ever slept. Belsomra didn't help, let alone lowly melatonin or lavender.

His name is Morpheus. Not the character from *The Matrix,* but the Greek godling of dreams. The son of Sleep. A good match for the former daughter of Insomnia. She wonders sometimes what children they would have if they ever had sex. Would they run around in their sleep?

How he ended up in New York State or how he managed to look so young, she would never know. He won't tell, and Wikipedia is mum on the subject.

She knows how she ended up here, all the way from the city of Tula in Russia. She told him, but he didn't share back. She forgave him.

Now, she's always asleep, save for some quick bites, mostly stale pumpkin pie, and even quicker trips to the bathroom. Her pee is ash-colored, too, but it has been that way since her stepfather had moved in.

When they first met with Morpheus, after she ran away from home, she introduced herself. "I'm Zolushka. It means Cinderella in Russian."

"I'm Morpheus. It means 'fashioner' in Greek."

"You are into fashion?"

They speak in English. She hasn't been long enough in America to tell if he has an accent. She knows she has a strong one.

"I used to be married to a prince," she said. "I was a mail bride. He brought me to America. We divorced. Princes can be jerks."

"Tell me about it, Pumpkin. I've seen a few. They snore."

Zolushka and Morpheus don't talk anymore. She doesn't complain. She doesn't care that opportunistic mice gnaw on her best friend, teddy bear Misha, whom she brought with her from home. She ignores the increasingly urgent emails from her godfather Boris back in Tula, who had introduced her to her prince, and who demands she would wire him $100 through Western Union.

Zolushka's busy half-sleeping. She dreams about her prince. He never hit her. His was too refined. He tortured her with words. Unless she didn't quite get his English. It was also too refined for her. He made fun of her accent. Every time she woke up, she would find the prince sitting in his chair, staring at her. She began to be afraid of falling asleep.

When she met Morpheus, she also had feared at first because Morpheus never slept either, but she stopped worrying because his eyes were always closed, and his curly hair covered his pillow so prettily. After that, she was afraid that one night she would fall asleep so deeply that she wouldn't ever awake. Now, she's not afraid of that any longer.

A godling is an upgrade from a prince.

The only thing of value she has left from the prince is a pair of slippers adorned with tiny glassy beads, adorable. She wears them to bed. When she's awake, she checks out the grandfather's clock in the corner. It's stuck at five minutes after midnight, day after day and night after night. She wonders if it's noon or dawn or sunset sometimes, but it's hard to tell since the room is always dark. Noon is overrated anyway. She dreams of being fully asleep in Morpheus' arms for ever and ever. They would be dead happily ever after.

At least she would. Though happiness is overrated, it's still the sweetest thing out there. Right next to a good night sleep.

Cinderella's Sister or the Bridge to Nowhere

The dentist says, "You're so quiet today." He was timeworn himself, but still younger than his patient, the old man in the chair.

The old man's mouth is stuffed with bloody gauze, so all he can do to show that he appreciates the joke is to flash the victory sign and stretch his lips into an unconvincing semblance of a smile. He's bleeding like an animal neither he nor the dentist would eat.

They both came to the U.S. from a different somewhere else, so they must communicate in English.

"My tees hurt, doctor."

"Open ze mous."

The dentist is trying to fashion a bridge for the old man. The bridge is off. The dentist wants to cut the old man's bone, so the bridge would fit. He must be thinking that the old man is Cinderella's sister who cut off her heel so that the glass shoe would fit. The old man calls it the bridge to nowhere.

"Trust me," the dentist says. "Dis bridge is forever."

The old man's shirt is spattered with blood. "Don't worry," he says when the dentist allows him to rinse. "I have anozer shirt."

The old man's mouth feels like the international space station: half of the teeth American and half Russian.

The dentist's receptionists are also lagging behind the old man in age, but not by much. Whenever he walks into the office, he smiles at them, and says, "Hello, ladies. How was your day so far?" They all love him forever.

The old man dies eventually. Not today, and not tomorrow, but in many years since the date when the bridge was finally opened for the food delivery traffic. Sometime after that, the bridge will separate from his jaw and fall out. The old man has taken this probability into account and asked to be buried with his phone. It has the newest NeverDie® battery.

The old man calls the dentist from his grave. They put him on hold, but a few months later, the dentist arrives with his receptionist, so she could charge the old man. It's a new receptionist, young and fit. The old man wonders what has happened to the old ones. He has trouble speaking without the bridge.

The receptionist holds a wilted bouquet. A patient has probably brought it to the office.

The dentist descends into the grave. He's huffing and puffing. It's clear he hasn't done this before. He's not one of those dentists who rob graves for the used gold crowns. In one hand, he carries a jar of his best, most reliable cement that holds forever. In the other, he's clutching the bouquet.

He says, "You're so quiet today." The dentist is older than the old man now, because once you die, you stop aging, and the dentist is still alive. He removes the buried interstellar dust and the mortal remains of the dinosaurs from the bridge.

"It's like new now," he says, untangling himself from the grassroots and curious baby moles. "It will serve you well." His accent has much improved. He's practically a native now.

The old man flashes the victory sign and smiles. He has a photogenic smile with the bridge. All the receptionists said so. He waits for the new receptionist to confirm this. He's patient.

Mark Budman

Mark Budman is a first-generation immigrant. His writing has appeared or is forthcoming in *Catapult, Witness, Five Points, Guernica/PEN, American Scholar, Huffington Post, Mississippi Review, Virginia Quarterly*, and elsewhere. His novel *My Life at First Try* was published by Counterpoint Press. He has co-edited anthologies from Ooligan and Persea.